Their
Maze

Talia Quinn

There are so many things I want to say here, not that as a reader I usually spend any time on this section...

The first thing I really want to say is that this is a work of FICTION. I am a million percent here for the toxic, possessive, aggressive, dominating, and charming male characters that generally make up a dark romance. That being said, in REAL life, that shit is generally not OK. I'm saying generally here because I don't know you or your life; maybe you have a dark male lead in your life that is somehow, against literally all odds, not toxic. In which case, I'm beyond jealous and still think you should talk to a therapist in case you're wrong.

I'm not your mom, but if you find yourself in a toxic relationship, self-identified or maybe friends/family are telling you it is, PLEASE speak with a therapist and identify what are the healthiest options for you moving forward. In my experience, what gets my motor running in my imagination is not always what is best in reality. Of course, I'm not talking about consensual kink here.

In fact, I'm FULLY supportive of all healthy and consensual kinks. I promise to not yuck your yum, even if I don't understand it. As far as I'm concerned, if everyone involved is an adult, willing participant, and not fucking up their lives - all the power to them as my opinion really doesn't matter.

I guess this is the long, but not as long as it could have been, way of saying that I know some of the stuff in this book is toxic and I really hope you know it too. This book is NOT in any way, except maybe the empowering ways, meant to be an example of what you should strive for in a real relationship. It IS meant to make you hot and bothered, entertained, and hopefully interested in reading more of my content.

I can't thank you enough for giving my first novel the time of day and hopefully enjoying it! My friends and family seem to like it, though I didn't go into specifics on what my mom liked about it, so I'm hoping that means it's good and not JUST that they like me enough to read it.

I couldn't afford an editor or sensitivity reader, so any mistakes you see are purely my own. If you feel inclined, I'd definitely like to hear if I fucked something up. Like I said, the goal is for this book to be enjoyable for all who like this type of kink, so if I missed my mark and portrayed something in a harmful manner, I want to know and correct that as soon as possible.

I can't think of anything else to say, so I guess that means I'm done with the dedication or authors note - whatever this ended up being. Now onto the actual story!

Talia Quinn

Contents

Glossary

Pronunciations

- **A pheata**
  (uh fay-tuh)

- **A stór** (uh store)

- **Aengus Óg**
  (eng-us ohg)

- **Aes Sídhe**
  (aysh shee-uh)

- **An Cathair Ghríobháin**
  (un cah-hir gree-uh-vawn)

- **An Dagda**
  (un dag-duh)

- **An Morrígan**
  (un more-ee-gan)

- **Bean Sí** (ban shee)

- **Boann** (boh-an)

- **Bodb Derg**
  (bove jehrg)

- **Caer Ibormeith**
  (kayr ih-bor-mayth)

- **Craic** (crack)

- **Dunstan**
  (dun-stuhn)

- **Eald** (ee-ld)

- **Líadan** (lee-din)

- **Maelgwn**
  (mile-goon)

- **Mo bhanríon**
  (moh van-ree-uhn)

- **Mo bhuanghrá**
  (moh wang-raw)

- **Mo bod** (moh bod)

- **Mo mac óg**
  (moh mah-ck ohg)

- **Mo rí** (moh ree)

- **Mo shíorghra**
  (moh heer-uh-grah)

- **Mo sméar iúr**
  (moh smayr yoor)

- **Moira Boyne**
  (moy-ruh boyn)

- **Púca** (poo-kah)

- **Púcaí** (poo-kee)

- **Rígán** (ree-gahn)

- **Ronan** (roh-nohn)

- **Ruairidh**
  (roo-ahr-ee)

- **Samhain** (sow-in)

- **Sasanach**
  (sas-uh-nahkh)

- **Senán** (shen-awn)

- **Shillelagh**
  (shi-lay-lee)

- **Sorcha** (sor-kuh)

- **Súnáis** (soo-nawsh)

- **Súnás** (soo-naws)

- **Teàrlag** (chair-lahg)

- **Tír na nÓg**
  (teer nah nohg)

- **Túatha Dé Danann**
  (thoo-ah-ha day dah-nuhn)

Definitions

- **A pheata**: His pet.

- **A stór**: Dear.

- **Aes Sídhe**: The Irish term for a supernatural race of spirits known as fae in Celtic mythology, dwelling in an invisible world alongside humans.

- **An Cathair Ghríobháin**: The Maze.

- **Bean Sí**: Female spirits or fae in Irish folklore who foretell the death of a family member through screams, wails, shrieks, or keening.

- **Craic**: An enjoyable social activity; a good time.

- **Mo bhanríon**: My queen.

- **Mo bhuanghrá / shíorghra**: My eternal love.

- **Mo bod**: My penis.

- **Mo mac óg**: My young son.

- **Mo rí**: My king.

- **Mo sméar iúr**: My yew berry.

- **Púca** (singular) / **Púcaí** (plural): Celtic creatures of folklore believed to bring both good and bad fortune.

- **Rince fáda**: Irish long dance or rinka

- **Samhain**: A Gaelic festival occurring on November 1st, signifying the end of the harvest season and the onset of winter, also known as the "darker half" of the year.

- **Sasanach**: English or non-Gaelic person.

- **Shillelagh**: A wooden walking stick with a large knob at the top that may be used as a club.

- **Súnás** (singular) / **Súnáis** (plural): A sexual climax (e.g., orgasm).

- **Tír na nÓg**: One of the names for the Celtic Otherworld, a supernatural realm of eternal youth, beauty, health, abundance, and joy. It is often perilous or unfriendly towards human visitors.

- **Túatha Dé Dannan**: A supernatural race in Irish mythology, with many members believed to represent Gaelic deities.

Trigger Warnings

- Character Death
- Explicit Language
- Explicit Sexual Content
- Non-con Elements
- Age Difference
- Anal
- Anal Fingering
- Cunnilingus
- Emotional Slow Burn
- Fellatio
- Fluff and Angst
- Frottage
- Morally Ambiguous Character
- Multiple Orgasms
- Non-Consensual Blow Jobs
- Oral Sex
- Orgasm Delay / Denial
- Physical Fast Burn
- Possessive Behavior
- Rough Kissing
- Rough Oral Sex
- Rough Sex
- Vaginal Fingering

Prologue

~ An Morrígan[1] ~

I find myself oft intertwined with the realms of birth, death, and destiny, an intricate dance that has woven through the tapestry of my existence. Whispers, concealed behind the noble visage I bear, have bestowed upon me the mantle of a war goddess, as though such a title were one I did not ardently embrace. Yet, when those daring souls dare to address me directly, they hail me as their Great Queen, extolling my profound ties to the bountiful earth and the divine sovereignty it graciously bestows.

I stand as the embodiment of their land, its custodian and personification, for I have been entrusted with the essence of sovereignty. Deep within me, the bonds with sacred wells and celestial wisdom run, intricately entwined with the very fabric of my realm. It is this profound ability to peer into the harrowing demise of valiant warriors and shape the ebb and flow of warfare that compels the noble Túatha Dé Danann[2] to grace my regal abode all too frequently.

Yet, let us refrain from delving into matters beyond the scope of our present discourse, if you please.

In the days of my youth, when my spirit was but a tender bud, I found myself ensnared in the labyrinth of love, alas, a love unreciprocated. Cú Chulainn, the object of my deepest affection, held my heart captive, for I beheld him as a paragon of perfection in every conceivable manner.

---

[1] An Morrígan (un more-ee-gan).
[2] Túatha Dé Danann (thoo-ah-ha day dah-nuhn): A supernatural race in Irish mythology, with many members believed to represent Gaelic deities.

Alas, destiny did not grace my yearnings with its benevolence, and my fervent sentiments were met with silence, as he obstinately rejected my advances. Undeterred by his refusals, I embarked upon a multitude of endeavors to capture his attention, assuming various guises in each valiant pursuit. Whether as a sinuous eel, a fierce and cunning wolf, or a gentle bovine, bereft of its resplendent horns, he managed to inflict upon me considerable affliction. As an eel, my ribs were torn asunder, as a wolf, one of my eyes was deprived of its sight, and as a hornless heifer, one of my limbs suffered a grievous fracture.

To this very day, the reasoning behind his unwavering repudiation remains an enigmatic puzzle, causing great perplexity within the recesses of my bewildered soul.

In the end, I must humbly confess that an insatiable thirst for vengeance had consumed my being. The once fervent flame of affection that engulfed my heart had transmuted into an all-encompassing abhorrence, and I bear no remorse for the transgressions I enacted.

Reflecting upon the manner in which he treated me, I opted to materialize in the semblance of a venerable bovine and prophesied that his demise would coincide with the inaugural commemoration of my offspring's birth, a calf conceived during my halcyon days as a heifer. During my ultimate apparition to Cú Chulainn, I assumed the visage of a crow, perching with great import upon his steadfast shoulder. This guise, symbolic of the impending catastrophe that awaited him, served as an ominous portent of his impending fate.

Ultimately, he encountered his tragic demise at the hands of Lugaid mac Con Roi, a narrative deserving of a separate chronicle, for even the most indomitable of champions, such as he, could not evade the destiny I had foreseen.

Pray be assured, I beseech your noble patience as we embark upon this discourse together, for it carries a profound purpose.

In due time, I found myself bound in wedlock for reasons not of the heart's yearnings, but rather for matters of necessity.

Upon the sacred eve of Samhain[3], I rendezvoused with an Dagda[4], the illustrious leader of the esteemed Túatha Dé Danann, filled with eager anticipation for the impending clash against the abhorred Fomorians, our formidable mutual foe. In the aftermath of our encounter, I pledged to summon the sorcerers of Ireland, invoking their enchantments to vanquish the Fomorian monarch and strip him of his vital essence.

As I graced the battlefield, a solemn verse escaped my lips, promptly commencing the clash that thrust the Fomorians into the abysmal depths of the ocean. Following our resounding triumph, I recited yet another poem, extolling our victory and prophesying the cataclysmic demise of our world.

---

[3] Samhain (sow-in): A Gaelic festival occurring on November 1st, signifying the end of the harvest season and the onset of winter, also known as the "darker half" of the year.
[4] An Dagda (un dag-duh).

It goes without saying that henceforth I was excluded from sundry social gatherings. Let it not be proclaimed that I lack a sense of mirth, for indeed I possess it, albeit in measured abundance. However, it does indeed remain an undeniable truth that my pursuits primarily revolve around stirring warriors to engage in combat, instilling courage in my champions, and instilling fear in my adversaries, rather than entertaining them with merriment.

No matter how diligently I strive to safeguard the well-being of my people, both in matters of conflict and fertility, ensuring the protection of their territories and providing assistance, while utilizing my connection with the vast living cosmos to oversee our land and its creatures, it appears that all others solely fixate on my ability to divine impending doom, demise, or triumph in the midst of battle.

Indeed, this is the singular subject that occupies the thoughts of an Dagda when he seeks my guidance. Perhaps circumstances would have been altered had our union been forged through the bonds of affection.

An Dagda and I, indeed, have partaken in our fair share of amorous escapades, never feigning fidelity as an inherent principle of our arrangement. Thus, it is not due to his transgressions that I long to disentangle myself from his clutches. I have grown weary of this tether that binds me to him and his desires. I am ready to liberate myself from the vow I pledged to him countless eons ago.

Oh, how I yearn for the days spent in the company of my sisters and my beloved Bean Sí[5].

I now find myself poised to embrace the esteemed mantle of the Phantom Queen. To achieve such a noble quest, a multitude of intricate facets required a harmonious convergence, and it befell upon my humble self to deftly orchestrate them into a grandiose arrangement.

The creation of 'An Cathair Ghríobháin[6]', coupled with the fastidious endeavor to guarantee its eventual bestowal upon the youthful Moira[7], presented scant challenge in my path. However, the true examination of my fortitude lay in crafting something that would penetrate the depths of a tender young psyche, establishing unwavering roots within its tender grasp.

I was, of course, cognizant of the fated conflict that was bound to unfold betwixt Sorcha[8] and Rígán[9]. Sorcha, in her naive pursuit of an elevated existence, was destined to surrender her youthful brother, Ronan[10], to Rígán, the enigmatic king of the púcaí[11] in Tír na nÓg[12]. She would valiantly resist this preordained outcome, employing her

---

[5] Bean Sí (ban shee): Female spirits or fae in Irish folklore who foretell the death of a family member through wails, shrieks, or keening.
[6] An Cathair Ghríobháin (un cah-hir gree-uh-vawn): The Maze.
[7] Moira (moy-ruh).
[8] Sorcha (sor-kuh).
[9] Rígán (ree-gahn).
[10] Ronan (roh-nohn).
[11] Púcaí (poo-kee): Celtic creatures of folklore believed to bring both good and bad fortune.
[12] Tír na nÓg (teer nah nohg): One of the names for the Celtic Otherworld. It is often unfriendly towards human visitors.

allure to forge improbable alliances. Alas, Rígán would ultimately emerge triumphant.

To be perfectly frank, the intricacies of this held little import to me.

However, the embers of my curiosity were ignited by none other than Rígán himself, for he, in all his splendor, possessed a kindred spirit; a most extraordinary, inconceivable, and formidable bond with none other than Moira. The orchestration of their seamless union required the most scrupulous manipulation amidst the illustrious Túatha Dé Danann, yet its culmination bore the utmost weight and import, for it would herald the triumphant fulfillment of my majestic design.

Pray, allow me to expound upon the very essence of your presence here, that being the forthcoming tale of Moira and Rígán's amorous entwining.

Chapter One

~ Moira ~

I found myself again swimming, or rather drowning, in work. Being an attorney had always been my dream, and I had pursued it relentlessly. Which unintentionally made everything else in my life feel less important.

As my term was approaching its end, I questioned whether the sacrifices had been worth it. While I loved my job, some days it seemed like that was all I had. Who would I be if I wasn't Prosecuting Attorney Boyne[13]? The decision of whether to run again weighed heavily on me. In fact, I was almost past the point of needing to decide, according to my campaign manager.

I pushed a stray strand of my curly black hair behind my ear and let out a deep sigh.

"Moira," my assistant Sebastian called out, "you need to take a break. You've been at it for hours!"

I groaned and checked the time. As usual, he was right. I needed to get up, stretch, take a short walk, grab a snack, or do any number of things to prove that I knew how to maintain healthy work boundaries.

"I heard they're making a TV adaptation of 'An Cathair Ghríobháin'," Sebastian stated as he entered my office. In his forties, he had radiant olive skin, tousled blond hair, and brown eyes that leaned towards black. Even without his suit jacket on, he always looked sharp. "I know you want to talk about it."

I groaned once again; he knew me too well.

---

[13] Boyne (boyn).

There was no chance I would pass up discussing my favorite book or venting about my worries regarding the TV adaptation.

"I know you want to complain about how they're not going to pronounce the names the way your grandma did when she read it to you as a child," he baited. We might have had this conversation a few times before.

"If you already know what I'm going to say, what's there left to talk about?" I grumbled good-naturedly as I leaned back in my chair.

I knew I shouldn't have cared so much about a book, but it meant a lot to me. Perhaps it was because of my relationship with my grandma, my desire to feel connected to her Irish heritage, or the fact that Rígán was my first crush.

Most likely, it was just my nature to want others to be as precise as I pushed myself to be.

"How do you say the antagonist's name again?" Sebastian kept up his friendly taunting as he sat across my desk, "Wasn't it Ray-gan?"

"You know it's pronounced Ree-gahn," I ground out.

"And the girl is Sore-cha," he began.

"Sor-kuh." I realized he was deliberately provoking me.

Although, in all fairness, Sorcha was a challenging name for many Americans to comprehend. If it hadn't been for a native speaker repeatedly pronouncing the names to me, I would have never known how to say any of them. None of the people I knew would glance at Eald or Líadan and immediately think they sounded like Ee-ld and Lee-din.

"I think they're going to make it a romance," he drawled.

"Aaugh," I gagged. "Sorcha is 15 and Rígán is like 400, that would be so gross. And the book reiterated over and over that there was nothing romantic between them."

"Does a few years really matter to an immortal?" he joked. "Plus, it was probably a perfectly acceptable age back in the day."

"It was written in the 80's, pretty sure it was just as gross then," I insisted. Not that I hadn't fantasized about being with Rígán a million times, but that was obviously different.

"Let's go get dinner and I promise to agree with every thought you have about the adaptation and the book," Sebastian wheedled, obnoxiously batting his eyelashes at me.

"Go home Baz, there isn't anything else you can do here tonight and I have to finish up before I head out." While I knew he was right and dinner would be enjoyable, I couldn't leave without making some headway on my caseload.

I truly cared about pursuing justice and striving to create a slightly fairer world.

"You know you're working too much, right?" he sighed. "The world won't fall apart if you work less than 80 hrs. a week or took a night off."

"I do not work that much!" I protested.

"You really do!" he countered. "I've been keeping track. I know how much you like data and facts."

We stared at each other in silence. It was actually endearing that he cared so much, and I loved that our relationship was more than just professional.

Yet, we both knew I was too obstinate to go home until I felt good about it. I had a strong will and wasn't afraid to stand up for my beliefs, which made me a highly effective prosecutor.

However, these traits also posed challenges in various aspects of my life.

In my personal life, qualities like being organized, caring, imaginative, or composed had fewer downsides. I often wished I had more control over when these characteristics surfaced. It would have been nice to only feel compassion for those who deserved it or be more adaptable when it benefited me.

If anyone deserved my flexibility, it was Sebastian. He was everything I had always imagined a big brother to be. We had only worked together for a few years, but we treated each other like family. Honestly, working with him every day was the only thing I wasn't burnt out on at the time.

"I'm not going to run again," I blurted, not truly knowing that was how I felt until I said it out loud. "Shit, it felt good to say that and mean it."

"I am so glad to hear that," he crowed. "Not that I don't love having you as a boss, but you're somehow both too young and too old for this to be the only thing going on in your life. Plus, I hate how much of yourself you pour into every part of this job. There's going to be nothing left of you…"

"Damn, tell me how you really feel," I teased.

"So, dinner and drinks then?" he cajoled.

"Fine!" I relented; it was already Friday night. "I swear, you are the only one that ever beats me in an argument."

"Only because you let me," he sang.

He was right, of course. If I didn't trust that he was looking out for me, I would never give him an inch.

I stood up and stretched, realizing that I needed to do it more often.

I smoothed out the skirt on my dark teal wrap dress and Sebastian grabbed my charcoal tailored blazer from the office closet. As I slipped out of my office slippers and into my leather ballet flats, he assisted me in putting on the blazer.

I contemplated whether to bring my laptop home or not.

"Leave it," he demanded.

"You're right," I acquiesced.

I grabbed my phone and purse, and followed him out of the office. I locked up, while he grabbed his things from his desk, and we headed out.

The autumn air had a pleasant temperature, so walking a block to our usual Cuban restaurant wasn't uncomfortable. I knew that in a few weeks, the Midwest would only be comfortable when indoors.

Sebastian texted as we walked, probably informing his partner that we were having dinner and drinks.

I didn't mind the lull in our conversation; the silence felt comforting and allowed me to contemplate my choice of not running again. I was filled with a mix of fear and immense relief as I embarked on a new chapter in my life.

The big question was, what would this chapter entail? What were my desires? Who did I aspire to become? I had no idea; I just knew I couldn't keep on the way I had been.

Sebastian held the door of Cubana open for me as we walked in.

I was immediately greeted by the mouth-watering aromas of garlic, onions, green peppers, black beans, and spices. The restaurant was adorned with colorful artwork, showcasing scenes of Havana and iconic Cuban landmarks. The walls resonated with lively music and the sounds of laughter and conversations, in both English and Spanish, filled the space.

The warm, friendly atmosphere immediately put me at ease, each visit felt like a reunion with old friends.

My stomach let out a loud growl, reminding me that I was famished.

"Let's grab a booth," I suggested and we headed towards an empty one.

"Are you going to try something new this time?" Sebastian asked.

"You know I'm not," I groaned. "I want to try something else, but what if I hate it? Then what would I do? Better to just get what I know I love."

Sebastian rolled his eyes as we sat across from each other. "You're ridiculous. You love trying new things but then stick to the first thing you like."

I shrugged; it had worked pretty well for me so far. If I ever got tired of Arroz con Pollo, then I'd try something else.

It really wasn't that deep... probably. Besides, he got Lechon Asado more often than not.

"Mind if Lex joins us?" he asked.

"Of course not, but can we order for him now?" I begged. "I'm starved all of a sudden."

"Sure," he chuckled.

~ Alexander ~

I loved it when Sebastian convinced Moira to join us for drinks. She was a riot when she let loose. Not that she wasn't fun otherwise, but she often appeared preoccupied with her career.

I smiled as I entered the cozy atmosphere of Cubana; tonight was bound to be enjoyable.

I caught sight of Sebastian first, unable to ignore the presence of the most handsome man in the restaurant. He seemed almost giddy while talking with Moira, and I couldn't help but wonder how many drinks they had already enjoyed.

Moira's face was radiant, her porcelain skin flushed, and her blue eyes sparkled with laughter.

As if sensing my presence, Sebastian turned around, and our gazes met.

"Lex!" Sebastian called. "Over here!"

I strolled over and kissed Moira's forehead before settling down next to Sebastian.

We had been together for a decade, yet I remained utterly enamored with him. We never grew weary of each other's presence.

"Are we up to the Culto a la Vida yet?" I playfully teased, aware of their preference for trying a new cocktail with each round. Typically, the sequence would include Mojito, Bumbo, Cojito, and, if the night lasted long enough, Culto a la Vida.

"Gods, no," Moira reassured me.

"She's been taking forever to finish her Mojito," Sebastian mocked. "I've been ready to move on for ages. I just ordered the next round as you came in."

"I thought we were celebrating," I quipped.

"Oh?" she tittered. "Is that what he told you? I think most people celebrate when they win their campaign, not when they decide to forgo it all together."

"Eh." I shrugged. "I think we're celebrating someone in their mid-thirties finally deciding to focus on something other than their career. Maybe even act their age for once."

"Ope, that." She rolled her eyes and frowned a bit.

I could tell that she was getting too into her head, which was something that happened often. Based on what she had mentioned before, becoming a prosecutor had been a lifelong goal for her. When her parents passed away, and later on, her grandmother who raised her, it seemed like her ambitions were the anchor she held onto while grieving.

Our thoughts were interrupted as the drinks were served, saving us from further introspection. We spent the rest of our time together indulging in food, drinks, and talking about lighter topics.

~ Moira ~

The next day, my phone woke me up earlier than I found acceptable. I despised mornings and typically indulged in sleeping in and relaxing during my weekends, only working a little in the evenings. That's why being awakened at seven was even more devastating.

"Yeah?" I mumbled into the phone.

"We're outside, let us in!" Alexander prompted. "We're here to take you to the Farmers Market and then a celebratory brunch."

I knew they were both just trying to be supportive, but I couldn't celebrate anything until I had a plan that I could put in motion to move me towards whatever my next goal was.

Maybe I should have had at least one long-term relationship by then, not just a string of very satisfying fuck-buddies. Maybe even a kid or two? Did I even want kids? I had never really spent much time thinking about it.

"It's too damn early…" I whined. "I'm still sleeping."

"Nonsense," he argued. "We're already here, are you really going to leave us out on your porch?"

"Uggghhhh," I groaned and hung up.

I dragged myself out of bed and stumbled towards the front door. Bleary eyed, annoyed, and still in my pajamas, I opened the door to greet my guests.

Alexander always managed to look put together, even when he was wearing jeans and a Henley t-shirt, like today. He was in his late thirties and had glowing olive skin, undercut brown hair, and hazel eyes.

Sebastian looked equally wonderful in his white t-shirt and black leather pants.

I hated them; it was too early to be so awake and beautiful.

"Get in here," I grumbled. "I need to shower or something if we're going somewhere."

"Be quick," Sebastian pleaded. "I don't want to miss out on the egg rolls."

"Feel free to head out now," I countered with a mock glare.

I'd choose going back to bed over going to the Farmers Market. I knew I would need a gallon of coffee to make it through the morning.

I showered and then styled and diffused my medium length corkscrew curly hair. After that, I quickly applied the bare-minimum amount of makeup I needed to make myself feel semi-decent. I opted for my favorite outfit: black jeans, a heathered gray t-shirt, a fitted black moto jacket, and comfortable leather ankle boots.

In the end, it only took me about 30 minutes to get ready.

"Still want to go?" I questioned as I headed into the living room.

"Gods, yes!" Sebastian exclaimed. "Let's go already!"

"You heard him," Alexander joined in.

I couldn't help but smile.

Even though I was torn from my bed at an ungodly hour and denied relaxation, I loved spending time with them. Going to a dumb Farmers Market didn't matter because having them as my best friends was the best thing I had ever done.

~ Sebastian ~

I knew we were pushing Moira. I just couldn't help it; she was too cute when she was disgruntled, and it was so rare that she let anyone push her outside of her comfort zone.

I wanted to watch her grow and embrace life as she shed the weight of only living for her career. I wanted us to have traditions and habits that weren't work-related and were set in stone before we didn't work together anymore.

I didn't care if that made me selfish.

The Farmer's Market was a great place for Moira to meet new people and bulk up her social life a bit. Plus, with us there with her, it was more likely she'd actually talk to people.

We may have been checking out some of the vendors for her recently; it had been clear to me for a long time that she needed something more in her life than just work. I just needed her to figure that out too, before we started subtly introducing her to them.

At just a little past eight, the Farmers Market was already bustling with people. The vendors had arranged their stalls in an inner square surrounded by an outer rectangle. As we entered, we received maps that indicated there were stalls offering a wide range of local foods, beverages, meat, fruits, vegetables, plants, and homemade goods.

"I neeeeed some egg rolls in my life," I complained and urged the group to hurry towards the stall as fast as possible. They ran out of egg rolls so fast and we were already later than I had hoped for.

It was purely coincidental that the Wild Goat Farm stall, with the most attractive farmer I had ever laid eyes on, happened to be right next to it.

"I'm out on the egg roll," Moira stated. "Is there coffee around here somewhere?"

"Baz is going to have a melt down any second now," Alexander joked. "Let's get him his egg roll and then we'll take you to the best coffee vendor here."

"Fiiiiinnneee," she agreed.

We arrived just in time to grab the last few egg rolls.

But where was that damn cowboy looking, plaid wearing, brunette man bun sporting bastard? His stall was completely unmanned, pun intended, but set up nicely to display his goat milk, soaps, candles, and cheeses.

"Ope," she gasped, "I need some of that goat cheese in my life. Do you think the vendor will be back soon?"

Moira sampled some of the goat cheese and groaned in delight. We waited around a few minutes but he still wasn't back. I cursed our luck and resigned myself to bailing on our meeting today. Thankfully, I didn't believe in fate.

As we meandered towards the 45 Parallel Coffee stall, I thought about which stalls we should hit up next. There were only a few other options I really cared about socially and several that I thought she would enjoy perusing.

Plus, Alexander would want to pick up a week's worth of fresh fruits, vegetables, and flowers for the house before we left.

The kombucha brothers were probably the closest to the coffee vendor and seemed as good a place as not to go next.

"Lex," I murmured, "didn't you want some kombucha?"

"What, yes!" he replied. "I wanted to try their new flavor."

"Coffee first, you guys promised!" she demanded.

"Of course!" he chuckled. "It's actually just a few stalls down from the coffee one."

Moira got her basic bitch coffee that she loved, and we moved on to the Fitz's Fermented Fizzies stall.

Thankfully, the hipster with his long braided blond hair, easy smile, and mellow vibes was there. I worried he would be too relaxed for Moira, but sometimes your opposite is exactly what you need in a partner.

"I heard you had a new flavor," Alexander started, "something with strawberry?"

"Yeah," Fitz acknowledged, "Strawberry Jalapeño. It's killer."

"Do you make this all yourself?" Moira interjected.

"Yup," he grinned. "I don't usually give out samples, but tell me if there is one you want to try."

"Ope, I don't know," she balked, "I've got this huge coffee already…"

"He has a mojito flavor that you'd love," I interrupted.

"It's actually my favorite," Alexander joined in.

"Are you sure about samples?" Moira speculated.

"Definitely." Fitz opened one of the bottles of mojito kombucha and poured out a sample for her to try.

"Damn, that's really good!" she exclaimed with a wide smile. "Can I buy the rest of the bottle and get a six-pack? This is perfect for my lunches."

"This one's on the house," he indicated as he added the sample bottle to the others in a bag. "I put my card in there in case you have any questions. It's got my cell listed."

"Thanks so much." Moira blushed as she paid and accepted the package.

Things could not have been going better, in my humble opinion. However, the real hurdle would be Moira.

She didn't require assistance in attracting interested individuals, regardless of gender. What she did need help with was transitioning her interactions from casual flings to genuine relationships. Based on my observations and the things I'd heard, guys often vanished when they were repeatedly ignored due to her career or only contacted for sex.

"Wellll," Alexander snickered, "I'll still get that new one."

"Of course," Fitz agreed with a warm smile. "You'll have to tell me what you think."

Alexander paid for the bottle and took it. We waved and started walking, with Moira leading the way.

Alexander and I grinned at each other like lunatics while she wasn't looking. It was great to see a plan coming together, especially one that might make my friend very happy in the long run.

For the next couple hours, we wandered from stall-to-stall sampling, observing, and chatting. After we'd worked up an appetite, we decided to walk over to a local retro-diner. Today was turning out to be everything I could have hoped for.

The sidewalks were fairly deserted and the walk to Rustbelt wasn't difficult, but traffic at this time of day meant it might take a little while to get there. It was easy enough to fill the time with Alexander and Moira, we always had plenty to talk and laugh about.

I noticed Moira was getting antsy and pushing us to walk faster than normal. When we stopped at the next crosswalk, she seemed even more agitated.

"Everything okay?" Alexander looked at her with concern. "What's going on with you?"

"I think I drank too much coffee," she huffed. "I might just run ahead a bit to get to the bathroom."

"Ha," I snorted. "That'll teach ya."

She gave me some serious side-eye and took off at a brisk pace when the crosswalk signaled she could cross.

We leisurely set off behind her, with no intention of catching up. I wanted to savor the walk and cherish every moment of the unusually sunny fall day.

The bus wasn't supposed to be turning left into the crosswalk.

It felt like time had stopped and sped up simultaneously.

I screamed at her to move.

We had the right of way; this shouldn't be happening.

Moira was too far away for me to reach.

My body froze up as my heart raced.

By the time she saw the bus, she couldn't get out of the way.

Her lips were moving.

The screaming continued.

A sickening sound filled the air as the bus collided with her, followed by the impact of her body hitting the pavement.

I no longer knew how to breathe.

The front of the bus continued over her and then the back before it came to a stop.

Suddenly, everything went black.

Chapter Two

~ Moira ~

The last thing I remembered was pleading for the most unlikely source of assistance. In that moment, I knew I wouldn't be saved but a version of Sorcha's appeal still fell uselessly from my lips.

My last words were, "I wish Rígán would come and take me away."

Then it felt like I was floating, slipping in and out of consciousness, too dizzy to move.

Haunting harp music pulled at the edge of my awareness and a medley of tantalizing aromas wafted through the air.

Slowly, I came back to myself. It felt like I was laying on something hard, but it didn't feel like it was pavement, more like a polished floor. As the nausea and vertigo faded, my eyes drifted open to take in the surreal situation around me.

The room was filled with animal-masked dancers in vintage ballroom clothing. They all looked ridiculously ostentatious and resembled something straight out of Louis's French court. They were engaged in some kind of dance where men and women formed lines, dancing in place across from each other.

I focused on the details of the dance and dancers. When I let my mind wander back to what happened to me or started to think about what was really going on, it felt like my head would explode. I only seemed capable of anchoring myself in observing the minutiae of the present moment.

In the next part of the dance, sets of two couples joined hands in the center of the lines and promenaded clockwise. Then they repeated the dance, going counter clockwise.

The women wore extravagant silk dresses with scandalously low scooped off-the-shoulder necklines, adorned with lace collars. Their short-ruffled sleeves stopped at their elbows, and their long-embroidered bodices were tightly corseted. The full skirts featured long trains and contrasting petticoats.

Their hairstyles consisted of a large oval bun woven with ribbon at the back of their heads, with an abundance of loose curls framing their faces.

The more I allowed myself to soak in the absurdity of the moment, the better I felt. My head stopped throbbing and I was able to push myself to a sitting position.

Next, every other couple danced down the line between the remaining couples, turned around, danced back to their original place in line, circled around the same gendered member of the couple who hadn't danced the line yet, and switched places in line.

The men's fashion was remarkably flamboyant, with low-heeled shoes, baggy breeches, long-sleeved coats, sleeveless vests in contrasting colors, and ruffled long-sleeved white shirts. Ribbons were looped through every available spot on the lower parts of their sleeves and shoulders.

The men wore their hair long, parted in the middle, and cascading down in elegant curls around their shoulders.

I chanced a moments reflection to consider how I felt so objectively normal. The last real thing I could remember was the Farmer's Market. Was I really hit by a bus? How did I end up in this odd ballroom? Why did I feel physically better by the moment? When the stabbing headache reemerged, I shifted back to the scene in front of me.

All the couples had gathered in the middle, joined hands, and swung around with their partners across the floor several times before lining up again. The dance seemed to go on forever, giving every couple a chance to dance down the center.

The longer I watched them dance, the less human they seemed. Something was off with the way they moved. Perhaps it was the shapes of their bodies. I couldn't quite put my finger on it. Everything seemed so dreamlike it was hard to be bothered with figuring it out.

~ Rígán ~

I clocked her the second she was brought into the ballroom. Her fragrance was unlike any other, a mix of sweet lavender, wild bluebells, and warm vanilla.

Despite the lively dance to An Caiptín Ó Catháin's rince fáda, I couldn't help but steal glances at her. She seemed completely lost, taking in the room as if she were in a trance. She lay on the floor for an unreasonable amount of time

31

before sitting up. Then she just kept sitting there for what felt like an eternity, staring into space. Finally, she got up and appeared to shake herself free of her trance.

She wasn't the same as I remembered. Something felt off, but every time I tried to pin it down, the thought slipped away. Someone else was involved, and that was unacceptable. This was my domain, and I alone ruled it.

It was bleeding hard to stay angry as I kept eyeballing her. She was a fecking vision of pure beauty, like something outta another realm altogether, taking hold of my very soul.

Her deadly figure, with curves that threatened to burst outta her shimmering silver modernized baroque gown, had me enchanted. Her porcelain skin, touched by a delicate rosy hue, was radiant and had a right pull on me. Them mesmerizing blue eyes were drawing me in like a bleeding magnet. Her full lips, like a delicate petal, were beckoning me to taste their sweetness.

The way she carried herself, all confident, made it crystal clear that she owned her own beauty.

But it was her amazing curvaceous form, lovingly embraced by the posh gown with dark opal details, that right stole my breath away. I hadn't recalled her figure being so exquisitely feminine, like every curve and line whispering of her strength and grace. Her physique, with its captivating roundness and gentle curves, lit a fire in me that couldn't be contained.

A deadly silver diadem with white opals graced her head, and her black hair was styled in meticulously arranged curls and ringlets, all mixed with shimmering beads.

I was mesmerized by her, like nothing I ever felt before. The urge to reach out and touch her, just to make sure she was real, was overwhelming. I had to hear her voice and see her smile, like I needed air to breathe.

~ Moira ~

My head was clear and as long as I stayed away from thinking too hard about how I got here, I finally felt completely fine.

My mind wandered, as it often did, to a familiar scene in 'An Cathair Ghríobháin'. I recalled the moment when Sorcha clumsily snuck into Rígán's grand ballroom. It was one of my favorite parts of the book, partly due to the exquisite descriptions of Sorcha's dress and the enchanting portrayal of Rígán's handsomeness.

However, even I, fan-girl that I was, realized that not much of significance transpired during that chapter. What always stood out to me was how the author meticulously detailed the dance steps and everyone's attire, only for it to ultimately hold little consequence in the larger narrative.

At that moment, uncertainty plagued my mind. I itched to move, to shake off the feelings of anxiety crushing my chest. Reality blurred, and I found myself questioning the authenticity of my senses and memories.

I couldn't remain idle any longer; I needed to unravel the mystery unfolding around me.

If this was a dream, I wanted to experience it. I wanted to focus on anything other than the fear of what happened to me before I arrived here. If this was reality, which it couldn't be, I needed to get the hell out of here and back home or to a psych ward.

I walked further into the room, mindful to not disturb the never-ending dance. The dancers stared at me and acknowledged my presence through careful avoidance. I didn't know what I would do if I had to interact with any of them.

I cast my eyes away from the dancers, trying to focus on the ornate details that surrounded me. The grandeur of the room, with its exaggerated architecture and lavish decor, only heightened the surreal atmosphere that enveloped me.

The ceiling had an intricate domed design that called to me, but I was too distracted to stare at it for long. The room was packed to the brim with so much to look at, I couldn't keep my eyes from quickly wandering from one sight to another.

I ran my fingertips along the rows of majestic columns, that felt much too real for a dream, as I further explored the room. Vibrant three-dimensional murals seemed to come alive on the walls, enticing my gaze. Boldly contrasted

paintings demanded attention, pulling me further along the walls of the ballroom.

I caught another whiff of the mouthwatering delicacies that had been artfully prepared for the occasion. Intertwined with the savory scents, the air carried the scent of freshly baked pastries and chocolate. I wondered if the food would taste as delightful as it smelled. Deciding to find out, I walked with more purpose along the outside of the room trying to find the source of the delicious aromas.

The silk wall coverings tantalized my fingertips, but I deliberately chose not to indulge in their tactile allure. Who knew how fragile they were. The ornamental brocade furniture I passed exuded an air of extravagance, but looked less than comfortable. I couldn't imagine spending much time seated upon their stiff cushions. The fur rugs, spread in front of oversized fireplaces, invited me to sink my feet into their plushness, but I resisted the temptation, remaining steadfast in my quest.

"Céad míle fáilte. An féidir liom an rince seo a bheith agam?"[14] A distinctly masculine voice, with a deep Irish accent, spoke from directly behind me.

"Ope," I gasped, caught off guard, and quickly spun to face him.

Thankfully, I was still wearing flats. Otherwise, I might have found myself sprawled on the floor in my haste to see who'd addressed me.

Tall and commanding, he stood about six and a half feet tall. Appearing to be in his forties, he possessed an air of confidence that radiated from every pore.

My heart pounded in my chest as I prepared to run or fight. I never expected that freezing would be my reaction.

"Tá tú an-álainn, mo chailín daor,"[15] he drawled and I couldn't help but gawk.

He was undeniably handsome, with bronze brown skin and hooded golden eyes that seemed to spark with mischief. All of which was generally enough to capture my attention, but he, quite inexplicably, had bull horns, ears, and a tail.

---

[14] Welcome. Can I have this dance?
[15] You are very beautiful, my dear girl.

They looked real, a fact my brain was incapable of processing.

His horns, curving beautifully from his head, seemed to crown him with an aura of untamed power and royalty. Their smooth, polished surface reflected the flickering light of the candlelit room, adding to his already breathtaking and otherworldly form. Waves of thick, black hair cascaded down his broad shoulders with an unruly charm, like he was just a bit too free to be truly civil. His ears were elegantly pointed and partially hidden beneath his hair.

His sensual lips were expertly curved and seemed to whisper promises of unspoken secrets. And beneath the well-maintained stubble that adorned his jawline, there lay a rugged masculinity that only amplified his immense appeal.

And then there was his tail, swaying gently with an almost hypnotic grace. It was as if he embodied the very essence of wildness and sensuality.

He wore a more modern version of the fashion seen in the ballroom, devoid of the ridiculous ribbons and embellishments, and he exuded an effortless elegance. That or maybe I was too preoccupied with the revealingly tight breeches he wore, that hugged his form leaving little to the imagination, to pay attention to the rest of his outfit.

"Huh?" I floundered as my mind finally caught up to the moment. "I didn't catch that. What did you say?"

"Feck, a Sasanach[16] stunner," he sneered.

---

[16] Sasanach (sas-uh-nahkh): English or non-Gaelic person.

38

His gaze lowered from my face and I blushed as I guessed what he was brazenly ogling. Clearly, turnabout was fair play. I tensed, unsure of how to respond.

Fuck this. It wasn't in my nature to allow someone to make me feel intimidated.

This conversation was going nowhere and it was time to leave, regardless of the heat spreading through my core. I squared my shoulders, held my head high, and forced my face to display complete indifference to his presence. More than one opposing counsel had lost their audacity after attempting to scorn me.

I turned to leave and he firmly grabbed my wrist. Goosebumps emanated from where he touched me and I shivered as the sensation flicked through my system.

Our eyes locked and I lost the capacity to think. In that moment, he was everything.

~ Rígán ~

Why did I remember her eyes as just green? Jaysus, her eyes were a fierce shade of blue-green with a tight burst of gold popping from her pupils.

For a second, when I first touched her, there was a spark, but then she went back to not giving a shite, which made me boil with rage.

Looking back, I had dismissed her as an insignificant creature, a somachán, unworthy of much consideration. I distinctly remember deeming her too old to be transformed into a púca[17], yet too youthful to hold any real interest for me. And I remembered her being Irish, though it was clear she wasn't.

My sole objective had been to have a bit of craic[18] before turning her brother into a púca. Yet now, my desires had evolved; I craved something far greater. But before anything else, I needed to uncover who the feck had dared to meddle in my realm and their motivations for doing so.

"Something's fecking changed about you," I seethed. "Perhaps you'd be so kind as to enlighten me on the cause."

She deftly wrenched her arm from my grasp, and I released it with a heavy heart. Her eyebrows furrowed adorably, and she peered intently at my gob. What shite was she pondering? Why did it bother me so much?

"I'm really not in the mood for whatever this is," she said, gesturing towards me.

She again impertinently tried to leave, and before I could think, I pulled her into the rince fáda with me. She resisted, struggling against my hold as we danced amidst my other

---

[17] Púca (poo-kah): Celtic creatures of folklore believed to bring both good and bad fortune.
[18] Craic (crack): An enjoyable social activity; a good time.

guests. No one had ever fought me while dancing before and I found it rather irritating.

"Rince liom, Sorcha," I coaxed, flashing my most charming smile. "I'll be bleeding knackered if you don't let me dance with the finest lass in this room."

Her demeanor softened, and she stopped resisting my advances. It was a relief when she finally gave in to my charms.

As we danced, everything else in the room seemed to fade away, leaving only the two of us in that moment. I knew I should be cautious, but I couldn't bring myself to give a damn about anything else at that moment.

~ Moira ~

This was a fantasy I'd had many iterations of before. None quite as detailed as this and Rígán seemed different than I normally imagined him, but once he called me Sorcha, I knew I was lucid dreaming.

Here, nothing could harm me; nothing was real. I knew I would eventually wake up and everything would go back to how it was before. I planned on enjoying this as much as possible before that happened.

I smiled and soaked in his unnatural beauty. He only had eyes for me, never looking away. I was equally enthralled. As always, I was irresistibly drawn to him in every aspect. Throughout the years, I had imagined him to be the perfect man.

I was thankful I'd spent so much time watching the dancers as I now knew what was expected of me. Rígán, of course, was wonderfully graceful and flowed through each step with ease. For my part, I did my best to just follow his lead and not focus on the couple times I stepped on his foot.

"I wish I could stay in this reverie with you forever." There was no reason for me to hold back or feel embarrassed in a dream. That was the best thing about being in love with a fictional man, they could never disappoint you or need more than you could give. They were only ever what you wanted at the moment. "It's only ever been you that I ached for."

His eyes widened for a split second before his smile did. Satisfaction seemed to roll off of him in waves, pulling me deeper under his spell.

There was nothing I wanted more than for him to kiss me.

I yearned for the moments I was close enough to be enveloped in his scent; reminiscent of Earl Grey tea, clover fields, and a seductive musk.

"Stay in this dream with me, Sorcha," he commanded, promenading with me down the center line. "Forget everything else and stay here."

I sighed bitterly, reminded that promises meant nothing in a dream. I was bound to wake up soon and we hadn't even kissed. This was turning out to be the most realistic and disappointing fantasy yet.

The longer we danced, the more everything else in the room faded away. I no longer noticed the delicious aromas, heard the chatter of the other guests, or saw anything but Rígán. As was often the case in dreams, time no longer held sway over me. It could have been just the two of us there, beautifully coming together and apart, over and over again for eternity.

Rígán pulled me into a tight embrace and I impulsively leaned into him. I could feel the heat radiating from his chest and I looked up at him in anticipation. This was finally it.

As he lowered his face towards mine, I pushed up on my tiptoes. Our mouths met and I was immediately adrift in the sensation. His lips moved slowly over mine, his hands at my waist pulling me into him even closer.

I surrendered to him, feeling every imposing contour of his body.

His kisses grew more heated, his tongue plunging into me at his first opportunity. I moaned, losing myself in the fervor, forgetting how to breathe. My imagination had never been so profoundly visceral before.

I whimpered as I was forced to break the kiss. If it hadn't been for the lack of oxygen, I would have laughed when I heard him actually growl.

His hand moved to the back of my neck and pulled me into another kiss. He kissed me like he owned me; controlling, fierce, and passionate. I had never been more turned on, I felt like I was on the verge of combustion.

But reality intervened as the clock struck nine and abruptly the continuous music stopped.

My mind cleared as if coming out of a daze.

The other guests had closely surrounded us, their breath on my neck, and leering gazes unsettling. I gasped, choking on my fear, when I realized they'd never been wearing masks.

Their faces were bizarrely beautiful fusions that merged human and animal features into one. What initially appeared to be decorative feathers, fur, or scales were, upon closer examination, their very own faces.

My pulse raced as I suspected my dream was shifting into a nightmare.

Rígán sought my lips again, but I couldn't ignore what was happening around us.

"I can't stay here," I grunted as I struggled to extract myself from his embrace. "Something's not right about this place."

"Stop do streachailt!"[19] Rígán huffed, continuing to pin me against him.

"Let me go right now!" I roared back at him, pushing against his chest.

"Ní ligfidh mé duit imeacht,"[20] he snarled.

"I know you can speak English!" I thundered.

He had the gall to smirk at me.

Fear and anger pushed me to act and poisoned my judgment. I refused to be kept against my will and wanted nothing to do with these aberrations.

Summoning my strength, I reared back and kneed him in the groin with all my might.

~ Rígán ~

Jaysus, the pain was shite like nothing I'd ever felt before. I let out a bellow and collapsed to my knees, trying not to spew my guts up.

---

[19] Stop your struggle!
[20] I won't let you go.

No one had ever been bollocksy enough to attack me like that. My heart was hammering in my chest as I went berserk.

But even in my rage, I noticed she'd already scarpered to the other side of the ballroom. My guests were keeping well away from the pair of us, probably to avoid getting caught in the crossfire of my wrath.

She was scanning the walls for an exit. I needed to get her the feck out of here before I lost it completely. She was bleeding lucky she was the best ride of my life.

This wasn't gonna end here, not by a long shot.

But I could afford to bide my time for a bit o' sweet revenge. If I wanted to quench my thirst for payback, I had to get my shite together and prepare properly.

~ Moira ~

I was trapped in this garish, nightmare of a ballroom.

I felt bad about hurting Rígán, only somewhat less than I regretted we hadn't made it further before things got scary. But, it was hard to feel terrible about putting your needs first in a dream. I should have felt the same about the terror coursing through me, but I wasn't there yet.

Suddenly, it felt as if someone struck me in the chest, and I lost my breath. I tumbled head-over-heels, disoriented and liberated from the grasp of gravity. I careened through darkness, completely out of control, struggling to regain my breath.

Eventually, I hit the ground with force, miraculously avoiding any injuries.

As I recovered, I lay there for what seemed like an eternity. My body felt sore in a way that shouldn't be possible in a dream. Why hadn't I woken up?

Gradually, I was able to concentrate on something besides myself.

The darkness enveloped the surroundings more than I had expected, and a chill ran through me, not caused by the temperature, for it was actually quite mild, but rather by the realization that I had been dumped into a graveyard.

Every tombstone in sight was adorned with flickering lanterns, casting a gentle glow all around. Yet, what intrigued me most were the objects scattered among the gravestones. Here, in this ethereal place, lay remnants of each person's life.

Even more peculiar, if that was possible, I was back in the outfit I had worn to the Farmers Market; the clothes I had died in.

Fuck, was this hell?

Chapter Three

~ Moira ~

I wasn't certain about many things at that moment, but I knew without a doubt that I had entered the next chapter of 'An Cathair Ghríobháin'. Why or how I was here, I had no explanation for, but here I was.

The cemetery sprawled around me, nestled beautifully within the rolling hills. This place seemed to exude an air of enchantment. As if time itself had slowed down in deference to the departed souls who found their eternal rest here.

Amidst the gentle rustling of leaves, a soft breeze whispered through the cemetery. A subtle earthy aroma mingled with the evening air; carrying the scent of moist soil and decaying leaves.

As I surveyed my surroundings, I took in the rows of timeworn graves and archaic tombs stretched out before me. Some were plain and simple, while others displayed intricate details and loving craftsmanship.

I'd spent too much time in cemeteries to not understand how each of these weathered stones stood as silent witnesses to the stories ever so succinctly engraved upon them. The dates and names engraved upon my families' memorials meant so much to me and yet close to nothing to a stranger.

Nature had also claimed its place here, adding its touch of eerie beauty. Moss clung to tombstones and wildflowers bloomed amidst the ancient remains. In the distance, I could hear the occasional hoot of an owl, its haunting voice echoing across the cemetery.

In the story, this chapter was when Sorcha came to the obvious conclusion that her material possessions were less important than getting her little brother, Ronan, back from Rígán. I wondered if that knowledge would help my situation in any way.

As I surveyed the cemetery, a stray thought caused my heart to quicken, for somewhere amidst the tombstones and burial mounds, Líadan[21], the eccentric púca, must surely be lurking. Images of her peculiar form played in my mind; a curious fusion of a hunched elderly woman and a spiky hedgehog.

According to 'An Cathair Ghríobháin', púcaí were mischievous creatures that could be unpleasant or helpful

---

[21] Líadan (lee-din).

depending on their innate nature. They could take on almost any shape, grotesque or appealing, but always retained some sort of animal-like feature and golden eyes.

In the book, Líadan's hazelnut skin and aged face was etched with wrinkles that spoke of ancient wisdom. However, it was her golden eyes that truly hinted at her strange nature. Personally, regardless of the author's opinion, it always struck me that the hedgehog like spines emerging from her back more than hinted at her 'strange nature'.

I imagined her scuttling about, burdened with an assortment of treasured objects that she held dear. A humped back a testament to the weight of the peculiar possessions she kept pinned to her with her prickly spines. I'd always found her to be an oddly sympathetic creature, so attached to her worldly possessions that she often missed out on experiencing her actual life.

With renewed determination, I scoured the cemetery, hoping to catch a glimpse of Líadan amidst the tombs. However, I soon came to realize that searching for her was a futile and exhausting endeavor. If my favorite book was to be trusted, then the púcaí natural tendencies, elusive and illusive, meant she would reveal herself in her own time and manner.

I despised the waiting game, yearning for a more direct path forward. Frustration gnawed at me as I grappled with the reality that patience was my only recourse. If I was somehow inside 'An Cathair Ghríobháin', then I needed Líadan to move forward. I distracted myself by venturing deeper into the cemetery. The burial sites revealing the final resting places of both ordinary individuals and esteemed members of the community.

With each step, I marveled at the extraordinary assortment of objects laid to rest with the departed. I wasn't used to seeing so many material objects, outside of flower bouquets, residing alongside graves. It was as if they were preparing them for a grand journey to an unknown realm, ensuring they would be equipped with all they needed in their afterlife, or perhaps they were simply striving to ensure their loved ones' life, what made them unique, was never truly lost to time. Every item seemed to be meticulously chosen to serve as a testament to the deceased's status, character, and the profound respect bestowed upon them.

The larger tombs were brimming with a plethora of tools, spare clothing, grooming implements, and oil lamps. The burial chambers were adorned with additional garments, meticulously draped, creating an atmosphere of reverence and remembrance. I was shocked to see that some of the deceased were carefully positioned near magnificent chariots and wagons, instead of being interred.

As I continued to explore, hoping to find a way out without needing Líadan's guidance, I felt a deeper awareness of this society's beliefs and rituals. Each grave, with its unique composition of objects and positioning, seemed to speak to a culture that valued both material possessions and the intangible connection between the living and the dead.

Which was all very interesting, objectively. But my nerves were worn razor thin and I couldn't find it in me to be particularly interested in my surroundings or what they might contextually mean. I was caught between needing to distract myself to endure the wait and an overwhelming desire to run regardless of the fact I had no idea where I really was.

After what felt like hours of wandering and ceaseless contemplation of what'd occurred with Rígán, when I had all but given up waiting, a mound of dirt beside an open grave began to stir, capturing my attention. And then, like the dead rising from a grave, Líadan emerged from beneath the earth's embrace.

She snapped at me, in a thick Irish accent, like I had personally wronged her, "Sure, what's the craic? Why're ya just sittin' there, a pheata?"[22]

I almost laughed at the lack of pleasantries or slightest pretense she didn't know who I was.

"I'd like to find a way out," I attempted to say cordially, only really understanding some of what she said. "Preferably home."

"Do ya even know the way home?" she sniffed.

"Clearly not or I would be there already," I huffed.

"Ya wouldn't kick spuds to ducks," she chuckled.

The fuck did that mean?

'An Cathair Ghríobháin' was not exactly a cultural touchstone to Ireland, having been written by an American Celtic language professor that had never left her home state. So sure, it taught me some Irish phrases and pronunciations, but it in no way prepared me for actually conversing with anyone.

Líadan was successfully getting under my skin and I needed to regroup. Fighting with her would get me nowhere and I needed to get out of here.

I took the deepest of breaths.

"Would it be possible for you to help me find my way home?" I asked as politely as possible.

---

[22] A pheata (uh fay-tuh): His pet.

It was a struggle to be cordial as I was irritated beyond belief. However, all said and done, I felt I was handling this entirely preposterous situation pretty well.

"Ah sure, a pheata," she chortled, easily appeased. She preened as she looked over her should to take in the heaps of junk encumbering her back. "Everyone's lookin' for somethin'. Ya gotta have quick eyes like meself though."

"You're completely right," I cooed, reminding myself not to take my frustration out on someone who didn't have anything to do with it.

I wasn't actually mad at her and I knew she was supposed to genuinely love her clutter. I refused to lose sight of who I was, even if all of reality was apparently literally crumbling around me.

"Maybe ye're not as much of a gobshite as I thought," she trilled. "It's bleedin' impossible to find valuables like mine. Stick with me and I'll get ya started, a pheata. Ya won't have to go treasure huntin' alone."

I chose not to respond and followed her as she plodded along.

We often stopped so she could rifle through what the dead had left behind. It seemed impossible for her to put anything else on her back, but she somehow made it work with each new addition. She turned her nose up at a weather-beaten violin nestled gently on a moss-covered stone, its strings worn and wood aged. Yet, she seemed overjoyed when she came across an old hair tie.

Whenever Líadan was busy rooting through cluttered grave sites that held no interest to me, I walked amongst the graves. Unlike my earlier explorations, I was now able to focus on the meaning of the items I found at each site.

Each object revealed a different facet of a life lived; memories I could never access seemed etched into their very essence. In this hauntingly beautiful graveyard, the object left behind created a picture of humanity, reminding me of the profound complexity that defines all of us. I couldn't help but reflect on the fleeting nature of life. How easily we forget the significance of the everyday objects that shape our existence. And yet, they become the threads woven into the tapestry of our souls.

What material possessions would people think of when they remembered me? What would Baz and Lex leave at my graveside to tell the story of my life? Would it be the fountain pen I adored and kept at my desk, but never found the time to learn how to write with? I'd like it if it were letters from people I hope I'd helped along the way. Maybe it would be my favorite 'Opposing Counsel Tears' coffee mug that I used every morning.

My heart broke from the level of despair I felt when considering my life and possible lack thereof moving forward.

"Sorcha, I've stumbled upon a wee treasure for ya!" she called out, waving a handful of dead flowers.

"I'm not Sorcha," I sullenly tried to explain.

I knew how this part of the story went and I doubted following it would get me any closer to home. The thought left me bone tired and I could feel the prick of tears beginning to form.

If I could even go home…

If I was even still alive…

I needed to stop focusing on that, it was best to not get too stuck in the weeds of something I couldn't do anything about. I sucked in a deep breath and blinked away the tears threatening to fall. The best course of action I could take was to re-center, re-frame, and move forward with what I could control.

"Course ya are," she grumbled, throwing the dead plant at my feet, clearly put out. "Don't be actin' up, it's not nice to play tricks on yer elders. Hold on to your posies, a pheata, and keep your gob shut."

She lumbered forward, faster than I would have thought she could move. Every time I attempted to speak, she hushed me and grew even more agitated. We finally arrived at the lantern-lit tomb that held Sorcha's most cherished earthly possessions, as we both knew.

"Go on in there to see if there's anythin' ya like, a pheata." She pointed towards the tomb and tried to herd me inside.

We were clearly sticking to the script if Líadan had anything to do about it. It felt pointless to fight her.

I entered the tomb and found exactly what I had anticipated: Sorcha's treasured belongings. I walked around, observing the contents, meticulously organized, and each item in its special place. Nothing caught my attention as useful or significant. My search yielded no more than what any ordinary teenager might keep hidden away; notes, a diary, and smut, none of which would solve my problems.

Exiting the tomb, I unsurprisingly discovered Líadan waiting on the other side. Concern etched on her face, it was evident that she had been expecting me.

I sighed, knowing what was coming next.

"Aren't ya delighted to be home, a pheata?" she probed. "It's what ya wanted, isn't it? What about yer things, happy to have them back?"

When I didn't respond, she pushed her way into the tomb, examining and picking up various items. "There's nothin' out there for ya, a pheata. Best to stay where ye're put."

She began handing me random objects that Sorcha would have adored. Likely, Sorcha would have relished having all her possessions back, a chance to hide within these familiar confines. But none of this meant anything to me. My real concern was how long I should continue playing along with this charade.

I knew that soon enough, Ruairidh[23], Senán[24], and Maelgwn[25] would arrive to rescue Sorcha. Would joining them and following the story's plot benefit me? I wasn't sure I had much of a choice.

The book ended with Sorcha in Rígán's castle, and that was likely where I needed to find myself as well. I doubted any other place within this labyrinth would be of assistance, if there even existed a path back to my real life.

---

[23] Ruairidh (roo-ahr-ee).
[24] Senán (shen-awn).
[25] Maelgwn (mile-goon).

I wandered over to a wooden couch meant to cradle the departed, adorned with intricately detailed garments and delicate gold plating. Perhaps taking a nap and then deciding my next move would be worthwhile. Nothing felt so urgent that immediate action was required. A moment of rest might clear my thoughts and help me feel more centered.

Curling up and surrendering to sleep seemed fitting in that moment, so that's what I did.

Líadan continued to chatter about all of Sorcha's possessions and how wonderful it was to have them back. But I was exhausted in every possible way, and I needed a moment to let it all go. Her words faded into the background as I drifted off.

My dreams were shattered as I realized I was being crushed.

I jolted awake in complete darkness. Numerous objects pressed uncomfortably against me, pinning me to the couch. I struggled to free myself from beneath blankets, stuffed animals, trinkets, and clothing. I had no idea how long I had been asleep, but evidently, Líadan had piled everything in the tomb on top of me. Now it all lay scattered across the floor.

"The hell, Líadan!" I huffed in exasperation.

"Don't ya like to keep yer things close to ya, a pheata?" she queried, as if she had been helping me this entire time.

I rolled my eyes and stood, stretching my limbs and surveying the aftermath. She really had put about everything she could on top of me.

Finally, I heard voices outside of the tomb, calling for Sorcha.

The walls of the tomb started to tremble and crumble; dashing for the tomb door, I threw myself outside.

Ruairidh shook the tomb with all his might, his voice echoing through the air as he called out Sorcha's name.

He was a magnificent, fur-covered creature that looked like a fox, his coat a dark red, almost black color. His eyes blazed with a golden intensity as he thrashed against the tomb. Standing upright on his back legs, he had an imposing presence that evoked the likeness of an orangutan.

Senán perched atop Maelgwn, a majestic Irish wolfhound of immense size, his coat a striking gray.

Senán himself was petite, covered in short, dark brown fur, resembling a shrew. His golden eyes sparkled with a keen intelligence. Despite his small stature, he exuded an air of refinement, donning an elegant red military-style jerkin and a black cap adorned with a fashionable green plume. He held a staff in his hand, creating a whimsical picture of a young child pretending to be Robin Hood.

"Please stop!" I shouted over the din.

I didn't want Líadan to get hurt in all of the chaos. After all, she was just playing her role in all of this.

"A stór[26]," Senán observed, in his slight Irish accent. "At long last, we've found you and you've returned to us once more."

Ruairidh pulled me into a crushing hug. He spoke like a young child as he squealed in a Scottish accent, "Sorcha, we've fund ye!"

"I'm not Sorcha," I clarified as I gently extracted myself from his hug. "My name is Moira."

---

[26] A stór (uh store): Dear.

"What has transpired since our last encounter, a stór?" Senán inquired. "Ah, Sorcha, it is you indeed. I would recognize you anywhere."

"Really?" I asked incredulously. "I seem the same to you? You really don't notice a difference between me and a red-headed Irish teenager?"

"Nae, nae, nae!" Ruairidh thundered, stomping his feet. "Yer name's no Moira, it's Sorcha! Ye're giein' me a fright, quit it!"

"A stór," Senán scolded me, "what has come over you? Cease these foolish games that frighten poor Ruairidh so. We have a noble quest to which we must return! Do you not remember that you have a duty to save your dear little brother, Ronan?"

I sighed; this was not working. The more I fought the storyline the more agitated they became. What choice did I have but to play along?

~ Rígán ~

I'd gone back, like I did with Sorcha, to my favorite getup; a black cloak, long-sleeved open linen shirt, black waistcoat, gray pants, and boots.

Ronan was scampering around with the púcaí, while I lounged on my throne, soaking up the scene.

It'd been donkey's years since I last transformed a nipper into a púca. Even longer since anyone called on me to swipe a bairn. The púcaí needed new kin to continue to thrive.

Worse than that, I'd been fecking bored. A new púca would spice things up a bit, as they learned the ropes. It'd be deadly to see what shape they took and watch as they discovered their own peculiarities.

Those thoughts filled my noggin until Sorcha came along and flipped the game.

Boredom was a thing of the past. Sorcha had me captivated, and uncovering the culprit meddling in my territory became my top priority. A new púca could still bring a thrill, but it paled in comparison to what Sorcha had to offer. And the idea of punishing those foolish enough to cross my path brought a wicked grin to my face.

My attention was diverted to Líadan as she lumbered into the throne room. The way she avoided my gaze told me she had failed. Can't say I expected anything fecking different, really.

"Inis dom cad a tharla,"[27] I requested; needing to find out what had occurred.

"She was pure not feelin' the gaff or any of the loot in it," she sniffed. "I gave her all the deadly stuff to keep, but she wasn't arsed with any of it."

"An bhfuil aon rud aisteach cloiste nó feicthe agat?"[28] I probed; certain she had observed something peculiar about Sorcha.

"She kept bangin' on about not bein' Sorcha," she cackled. "Kept sayin' her name was Moira. I don't know what she's playin' at, to be honest."

"Aon rud eile?"[29] I questioned; she might have been withholding something.

"Nah, she's a bit of an eejit, but I didn't cop anything else," she remarked with a nonchalant shrug of her shoulders.

"Dea-obair, a Líadan,"[30] I muttered under my breath, lost in my own thoughts. It took me a solid minute before I realized she was still hanging about, waiting for me to bleeding dismiss her. "Is féidir leat a choinneáil ar fad a gcuid seoda."[31]

---

[27] Tell me what happened.
[28] Have you heard or seen anything strange?
[29] Anything else?
[30] Good job, Líadan.
[31] You can keep all her treasures.

She flashed me a grin that stretched from ear to ear as she scurried out of the chamber. Keeping her satisfied and loyal wasn't exactly rocket science. All she gave a toss about were her precious 'shinies'.

Sorcha, or maybe it was Moira, would be off with Senán, Ruairidh, and Maelgwn now. Sure, I was older and more powerful than the whole damn kingdom, maybe even all of them combined, but I had no interest in getting my hands dirty.

I preferred to outsmart rather than fight, especially when it came to her.

Maelgwn was still a wee pup, no threat to anyone yet. He was one of my newer púca, still finding his damn way and not even able to yap properly. Senán, on the other hand, was older than Maelgwn, but a proper bleeding gentleman who wouldn't cause a ruckus. Ruairidh wasn't much older than Maelgwn, but he was growing into his own skin faster. The lad had strength like a fecking ox, though he was too thick to use it for anything other than brute force.

None of her mates bothered me one bit.

"Teàrlag[32]! Dunstan[33]!" I bellowed for my generals, signaling that it was time to get ready for her grand entrance.

---

[32] Teàrlag (chair-lahg).
[33] Dunstan (dun-stuhn).

Chapter Four

~ Moira ~

"I guess we just need to head in there then," I said, more to myself than anyone else.

I stood there, taking in the surreal sight before me, and a mix of awe and disbelief washed over me.

The torch-lit gates of Púcaí City loomed tall and imposing, their weathered wooden structure giving them an ancient appearance. The design of the gates appeared deliberately chaotic, as if the architects had purposely defied all traditional gate norms, in a completely comical way. Jagged spikes stuck out at odd angles, serving as a deterrent to anyone daring enough to breach the city's defenses.

Yet, it was the púcaí faces adorning the gates that truly captured my attention. Painted with reckless abandon, their whimsical faces stared back at me with exaggerated expressions. As if each face seemed to mock anyone foolish enough to challenge the city's power. The artists had used a riot of colors, splashing vibrant hues onto the wooden surface.

From our vantage point atop the hill, concealed by lush greenery and shrubbery, my companions and I had a strategic advantage. We could see the púcaí guards stationed at the gate, their forms illuminated by the flickering torchlight.

They were adorned in ornate armor and armed with weapons, standing as sentinels, ready to protect their city at all costs. Their untamed aura and animalistic features added an eerie element to their presence.

As I surveyed the scene before me, I couldn't help but wonder about the city that lay beyond those ludicrous gates. What dangers awaited me within Púcaí City? Not that it probably mattered, the story seemed to want to play itself out regardless of what I did.

"We have arrived at the gates of Púcaí City, a stór," Senán boasted, raring to continue on. "Beyond lies the castle, the very object of your quest, as you have stated before."

"Yup," I groaned; it was one thing to know what was going to happen and another to actually live it and hope you prevailed as planned.

I couldn't help but wonder what Rígán was up to at that very moment. Was he still thinking about out kiss as much as I was? Had his actions also been predicated on the belief that I was Sorcha?

"Then onward!" Senán interrupted my thoughts as he spurred on Maelgwn, taking off towards the gates with zeal.

Ruairidh and I decided to take a more relaxed approach, trailing behind him at a leisurely pace. I was in no rush to deal with what I knew was coming. He appeared content just to be by my side, sharing this uncertain journey.

A faint hint of burning torches drifted towards me, their smoky fragrance tinged with a touch of sweetness, creating an ambiance both eerie and somehow inviting.

Senán, driven by his unyielding self-assurance, released his war cries, and bum rushed the gate itself. He was nothing if not confident in his own skills. I'd be more concerned if I didn't know he would survive all of this.

In the story, Sorcha had stopped Senán from waking the guards, but I doubted my lack of action would change much. After all, nothing I'd done so far had any impact on the overall plot.

"Open these gates!" he roared, as he ineffectively banged on them with the butt of his staff.

The guards watched him, nonplussed, seemingly unfazed by his display. The silence, broken only by nature's whispers and the occasional guard's movement, set my nerves ablaze.

"A stór," he squeaked in dismay as we reached him, "they have taken notice of me, yet they do not open the gates nor attempt to engage me in combat. If only they would charge, I would fight them to the death."

"I know," I reassured him, knowing just what he needed to hear. "You're quite brave and skilled in combat. In fact, I bet the guards are just afraid of you."

"But of course!" he easily agreed.

"Ruairidh, do you think you could open the gates?" I asked with a smile. "Since these guards seem too scared to deal with us?"

Ruairidh's dopey grin stretched across his face, radiating a pure, infectious joy, and I couldn't help but feel real affection for him. He effortlessly pulled against the gate, swinging them open without a hint of resistance. I couldn't help but wonder if they had even been locked in the first place.

As we passed through the gates, the guards watched our every move, but their presence felt utterly pointless in the grand scheme of things. They were well aware of what lay beyond the gates, just as I was.

The enormity of the situation loomed over me.

Initially hidden by the towering gates, the giantess now came into full view, and an overwhelming sense of terror washed over me. Her grotesque features seemed as if they had been plucked directly from the darkest corners of my nightmares.

Strands of blond hair, tangled and knotted, cascaded down to her broad shoulders. Her arms, thick as ancient tree trunks, hung menacingly at her sides, ready to strike at any moment. Sickly green skin covered her massive body, and her ragged clothes clung desperately to her figure.

The ground shook as she approached us, I could feel the bile inching up my throat. My pulse hammered and everything in me told me to run.

I knew we were supposed to win, but doubt gnawed at the edges of my confidence. So far it had proven true, but was I sure enough to face being crushed or worse?

Maelgwn, who I now considered to be the smartest of us all, took the fuck off.

Senán screamed at him to turn back and was forced to jump off when he didn't listen.

In stark contrast, Ruairidh remained calm in a way that suggested he didn't realize the trouble we were in.

"A stór, if that warrior and I were to engage in a joust with lances, I am quite certain I would make short work of her." Senán was clearly delusional and I wished I had an ounce of his bravado.

The giantess stood right in front of me now, casting a shadow that engulfed my trembling form.

My legs betrayed me, refusing to move an inch. I wasn't even sure how I was still standing. It was as if they had forgotten their purpose, leaving me stranded in a state of helplessness.

I watched the scene unfold as if I were an outsider, detached from my own body. I should have been running away screaming, instead I was the perfect impersonation of a fucking statue.

As her massive hand reached out towards me, I remained motionless, unable to do anything. My brain refused to process what was happening.

One moment I stood frozen, consumed by fear, and the next I found myself being lifted off the ground, tightly gripped around my waist. My arms were pinned firmly against my sides, leaving me defenseless.

Ruairidh and Senán, to their credit, were shouting and trying to get the giantess to put me down.

Darting in and out between her colossal legs, they skillfully evaded her powerful kicks while launching attacks whenever they could. Senán's staff proved futile, merely irritating her.

Ruairidh, however, managed to land fierce blows on her whenever he avoided being knocked down by her mighty punts.

Neither side seemed to be making any progress, but I was definitely getting whiplash from being swung around.

Any second now I was going to pass out or puke. I honestly wasn't sure which would be worse.

"Eald[34]!" Senán yelled pointing towards the top of the wall connected to the gates.

---

[34] Eald (ee-ld).

Everyone but the giantess attempted to look where he was pointing.

She instead took the opportunity to clear kick Senán over the outer gates. Senán's screams echoed around us as Eald ran across the wall towards the gates.

He had a peculiar appearance, resembling a dark-colored sheep mixed with an elderly man. His walnut skin was covered in wrinkles that almost obscured his golden eyes. He wore a coarse knit cap, a loose-fitting tan woolen tunic, and brown breeches that reached down to his calves. Notably, he went barefoot, revealing his hoofed feet.

It was finally time for Eald to turn the battle to our favor. At least that is what he was supposed to be doing.

Ruairidh continued to engage in combat with the giantess, who seemed oblivious to Eald's movements behind her. Through sheer luck or instinct, Ruairidh managed to maneuver her closer to the gates and Eald's position.

With impressive agility, Eald leapt onto the giantess's head, clinging to her hair for dear life. She swatted at him, but he skillfully evaded her blows.

Caught between Ruairidh's relentless assault and Eald's surprise attack, she struggled on two fronts and faltered.

Distracted as she was, Ruairidh delivered a devastating blow to her shin, the sound of her bone breaking piercing through the chaotic battle.

Enraged, she let out a wild scream, now solely focused on Ruairidh.

Seizing the perfect moment, Eald struck. Drawing a small dagger from his belt, he used the giantess's hair as a makeshift rope, descending from the top of her head.

Then he stabbed her right in the damn eye.

She, very understandably, lost her damn mind and her screeching sent chills down my spine.

Desperately trying to remove the dagger from her eye, she flung me aside in her frenzy.

I hit the ground hard, the wind was knocked out of me, and I promptly passed the hell out.

Darkness enveloped me. I must have only been out for a few moments, but when I regained consciousness, the giantess was gone.

Eald lay in a crumpled heap near the wall, while Ruairidh nonchalantly groomed himself. Senán and Maelgwn were still nowhere to be seen.

Groaning, I attempted to rise, every inch of my body throbbing with pain. I was certain I would be adorned with the most spectacular bruises. The back of my head ached terribly and the world swam, but I was able to get to a sitting position. Covered in sweat and dirt, vomiting was unfortunately still not out of the question. However, no other part of me seemed too beat up; surprisingly, my clothing had even mostly survived destruction.

"Eald," I croaked, my voice strained, "Are you okay? Ruairidh, maybe you should check on him?"

Ruairidh glanced at Eald but made no move to assist him.

I needed a moment to collect myself before attempting to stand, let alone move. I had to hope that Eald didn't require immediate help. I laid back down, too sore to continue sitting.

I roused as I heard someone or something coming through the gates.

Senán rode towards us on Maelgwn.

"We have returned, my dear fellows!" he cheered as they approached. "Pray tell, where is the monstrous giantess we set out to vanquish? Did we emerge triumphant? And why do I see everyone sprawled about in such an unseemly manner? Ah, but it gladdens my heart to see you safely returned to us, Eald, my valiant lad."

I was relieved to see that Senán appeared unharmed, clearly he was made of sturdier stuff than me.

"Wee Teàrlag skelped that big eejit and sent him fleein'," Ruairidh explained with a shrug.

What? I didn't understand what was being said here half the time.

Wait, who was Teàrlag? I'd never heard that name before. "Who's Teàrlag?"

"They're one of Rígán's bloody top-drawer commanders," Eald gasped out painfully, in a thick English accent, as he struggled to sit up. "They'd gladly catch a bullet for him without batting an eye."

"Ope, Eald," I asked again, sitting up as well. "Are you okay?

"I've had bloody worse days, but I'm alright," he grumbled. "Just to make it crystal, I ain't beggin' for forgiveness. Don't reckon I did all that just to be pardoned. I ain't ashamed of a bloody thing I did. I don't give a toss what you lot think of me. I told ya I was a blimmin' coward. Now ya see I was only speakin' the truth. And I couldn't care less about bein' mates with any of you bunch."

Well, he hadn't done anything to me. Sorcha, sure he kinda fucked her over a bit, but I understood why he'd behaved that way.

In "An Cathair Ghríobháin," Eald had disclosed Sorcha's whereabouts to Rígán after being threatened with harm. Being somewhat of a coward and unable to endure torture, Eald had immediately given her up and fled.

I had always suspected that Rígán was more interested in separating the two of them and leaving Sorcha vulnerable than in obtaining any real information from Eald. But that was not relevant at the moment. However, I wasn't about to hold a grudge over something I wasn't even a part of.

"All's forgiven on my end," I reassured him. "I'm not even Sorcha, so no need to dwell on anything."

"Nah, nah, nah!" Ruairidh immediately thundered, gearing up to throw a tantrum.

"A stór, not this again," Senán admonished. "My dear Ruairidh, there is no cause for concern. Sorcha is merely indulging in her whims again. And as for you, Eald, let us not dwell on the past. Our mission to rescue young Ronan still stands, and we must not be waylaid by misfortunes of the past."

"Honestly," I went on, "I would never have had the courage to stab anyone, let alone a giantess, in the eye. I don't think we'd have survived if it weren't for you."

"Verily, I must commend thee, dear Sir Eald!" Senán exclaimed, waving his staff about. "Seldom have I heard of such courage displayed on the battlefield. I dare say that even King Arthur himself would have been impressed by thy heroic deeds. We owe to thee our very lives, and in thee we see a true paragon of chivalry and gallantry."

Ruairidh looked over at Eald and gave him that lopsided grin of his. He was a beast of very few words. But at that moment, it seemed like Eald understood everything without needing a lengthy explanation.

"Are you lot forgiving me?" he nearly sobbed. "Seriously? Not that I give a toss about it or anythin'... but cheers anyways."

"Pray tell, what art thou waiting for?" Senán complained. "Maelgwn, venture forth! We must advance into the city to reach the castle posthaste!"

Without waiting for a response, Senán spurred Maelgwn forward, leaving the rest of us in his dust. I couldn't help but roll my eyes at his lack of consideration. Clearly, it didn't matter to him if the rest of us were exhausted and beaten to shit.

~ Rígán ~

"**D**'fhéadfadh sí a bheith gortaithe!"[35] I let out a deafening bellow, fearing that Moira had been injured, and I was just barely keeping myself from fecking tearing them apart, limb from limb.

My fists clenched and released; my mind consumed with visions of vengeance. The pure rage flowing through my veins could've set the bleeding sky ablaze.

Teàrlag was quaking in their boots, but they should've been shitting themselves with terror.

They resembled a colossal raven, with eyes that gleamed like polished gold, and their skin bore a dark hue. Their limbs were thin and spindly, and they stood at a meager height, no taller than a wee bairn.

I sauntered over to Ronan, giving Teàrlag a withering glare. The poor babe looked like he was about to soil his breeches. He was bawling his eyes out, so I scooped him up and held him close, trying to soothe him with a gentle bounce.

"Ah, she's pure belter, ya ken," Teàrlag grumbled in a Scottish accent, unaccustomed to feeling the brunt of my wrath. "The giantess took a right thumpin', mind ye, but I

---

[35] She could be hurt!

managed tae whisk her awa afore she caused any proper havoc. She'll need some heavy fixin', nae doot aboot it. As fur Sorcha, she didnae come aff too bad, she's sound as a pound. A' ends well, I reckon."

I was all set to unleash a fierce tongue-lashing, or perhaps even draw blood. My grip on Ronan tightened until he whimpered in pain. It was clear I needed someone else to keep an eye on him before I did something I'd regret.

"Tóg Ronan áit éigin eile agus coinnigh slán é,"[36] I swiveled and addressed Dunstan, transferring the wee one into his care.

He resembled a towering, shaggy badger with eyes that sparkled, standing upright on his hind legs. Despite his size, he was not much taller than Teàrlag.

Dunstan promptly whisked Ronan out of the throne chamber.

"Inis dom arís conas atá sí ceaptha a bheith ceart go leor[37]," I venomously hissed, prepared to lay all the blame on them for any harm that might have come to Moira. "Mura bhfuil sí i riocht foirfe, beidh ort buíochas a ghabháil leat féin as an fhulaingt."[38]

"Ah'm tellin' ye, she's pure braw!" they assured me. "Mibbe a wee bit scuffed, but that's aw! This wis yer notion, mind ye? It's no' ma fault the lassie couldnae haud oan tae her."

It had been an absolute donkey's age since I gave a feck about anything, and Teàrlag was doing feck all to soothe or steer my anger in the right direction. Right then and there, I couldn't believe why I had ever fancied them or put my trust in their sorry arse.

---

[36] Take Ronan somewhere else and keep him safe.
[37] Tell me again how she's supposed to be okay.
[38] If she is not in perfect condition, you will have to thank yourself for the suffering.

I strode over to my throne and slumped into it, needing space to deal with everything that had gone tits up and collect myself.

"Gach duine amach! Ní mór dom a bheith ina n-aonar!"[39] I roared, and the chamber emptied out in a trice.

She was never meant to cop a hurt. Sure, a bit scared, but no injuries. It was pure luck and Teàrlag's quick thinking that saved her. I put too much faith in them, they should have acted sooner. I wouldn't put her safety in anyone else's hands again.

I'd have the pair of them, her and Ronan, in no time at all.

Sure, I needed to isolate her from her chums; I craved her chained to my bed before the thirteenth hour chimed. But the main thing on my mind was how to make bleeding sure she was taken care of proper, like. I couldn't be settling for nothing less than making sure she was looking after, every step of the way.

And as for me, I wasn't about to be satisfied with anything other than getting my hands on everything I wanted.

---

[39] Everyone find out! I need to be alone!

Chapter Five

~ Moira ~

Púcaí City was an unusually colorful and vibrant place. The architecture of the buildings had a clear inspiration from nature. Tree branches and leaves were intricately woven into the design, creating a stunning blend of intentional construction and nature. As I passed by the houses, I couldn't help but notice the beautiful decorations adorning them; flowers of various shapes and colors

As I walked through its streets, it struck me how deserted it seemed, but the city still felt alive with its array of torches and lanterns that illuminated every surface. The wooden structures, standing tall on stilts, were connected by rope bridges, creating a fascinating network above the ground.

The fragrance of wood, blooming flowers, fresh foliage, and the subtle hint of water permeated the night air. Countless trees towered over the streets and foliage adorned every corner, filling the city with an abundance of greenery. The sound of water flowing could be heard throughout, as small streams and ponds meandered their way through the city.

A castle, presumably Rígán's, stood proudly atop a steep hill at the heart of the city. It was a breathtaking view that filled me with awe. It was made from imposing, massive gray stones, and the castle had an array of turrets, battlements, and spires. The architecture appeared somewhat disorganized and random, lacking a clear pattern or plan in its construction. Yet, I found this lack of conformity only served to heighten its unmistakable and captivating allure.

We easily walked through the city streets towards the castle.

If things continued to play out according to the story, we were about to be met by a púcaí horde that would chase us through the town until Sorcha made it to the castle alone. It was hard for me to believe that many púcaí were quietly lying in wait.

"I'm not fond of this eerie silence," Senán said, voicing what we were all feeling. "I had hoped for a worthy challenge. Where have all the warriors gone? It's not in my blood to wander through a deserted town when I'm ready for battle."

"Get a grip!" Eald complained. "You're just chatting nonsense."

"My apologies," Senán crowed. "I am unacquainted with the concept of fear."

We arrived at the city square without any hassle. All that was left was to climb the sharp path of stairs up to the castle. Then fight Rígán, save Ronan, and go home… nothing to it.

"That was dead easy," Eald exclaimed.

It was then that the púcaí flooded the streets and city square, their thunderous steps, bizarre shouts, and peculiar, furry figures overwhelmed me. We were surrounded, leaving no apparent path other than ascending the stairs into the castle.

I was surprised to see that none of them donned any armor or brandished any weapons; a clear deviation from what the book had described.

Although that was initially where I had intended to go, I now felt quite sure it was not the right choice. Fortunately, Eald knew the city better than the rest of us.

"Come on, let's leg it," he grunted and took off towards one of the stilted structures.

We followed him closely as he hurried up a concealed stairwell that could be accessed from the outside. By the time I managed to enter the building, he had already lit multiple lanterns.

"I'm a streetwise city slicker, know all the dodgy backstreets and the ins and outs of any place 'round 'ere," Eald explained with pride.

When we were all safely inside, what looked like a furniture shop for children, he quickly locked all the ways in and out.

"Ruairidh, can you push that wardrobe in front of the entrance we just came through?" I asked and he quickly complied.

The púcaí relentlessly pounded on every surface they could reach, the door, walls, shutters, anything they could find.

Unfortunately, there weren't any other large pieces of furniture we could use to block ways into the shop. This place didn't seem easy to defend, but was better than being completely surrounded outside.

"A stór, may I request that you and Eald guard the windows?" Senán commanded more than asked. "Maelgwn and I shall take care of the main entrance. Ruairidh, I implore you to ascend to the roof!"

We were all filled with uncertainty, but we obediently followed his instructions, desperately hoping that he had some sort of plan.

Personally, I was completely clueless about what steps to take next. However, in hindsight, I could have offered Ruairidh some guidance when he decided to reach the roof by literally going through it. I suppose the silver lining was that it wouldn't be a challenge to communicate with him, considering the gaping hole in the ceiling that now connected us.

As the púcaí finally tore off the shutters from the window frames, they began forcing their way inside.

Eald and I scrambled to defend ourselves, wielding whatever furniture we could find as makeshift weapons.

But their sheer numbers overwhelmed us. For every creature I managed to strike down with the shattered chair, two more would surge through the breached defenses.

Senán struggled valiantly with his small staff, but it proved insufficient against the onslaught.

Only Ruairidh seemed to hold his ground, fending off the encroaching horde, although even he was being engulfed by their relentless assault.

As the intense battle unfolded, it became apparent that the púcaí were gradually gaining the upper hand through attrition and their sheer numbers.

It was perplexing to witness their victory unfold, for it wasn't due to any form of retaliation on their part. Rather, they absorbed our assaults with an eerie calmness, their focus solely on evading Ruairidh's strikes.

Their peculiar strategy seemed solely aimed at encircling us, relentlessly attempting to occupy every available inch of space. In doing so, they effectively trapped us, leaving me with a profound sense of vulnerability.

"How cowardly!" Senán complained. "They won't face me in combat but instead let me try to break my staff over their heads. Is it even worth splintering my staff to dispatch the likes of you if you refuse to act like brave warriors?"

One of the larger badger-like púca shouted out in a British accent, "Why are you lot beefin' with 'er? We're all fam 'ere, you should be ridin' for our side! What 'ave we ever done to deserve this treatment?"

"You ain't done nuffin' to me or any of us, but you lot nicked 'er little bruv!" Eald explained.

"So, we pinched a kid! That's what we do, even you. You know that, Eald," the púca retorted.

Ruairidh crashed back through the ceiling, his body landing with a resounding thud amidst a shower of púcaí. The room fell into an abrupt silence, everyone startled by his sudden entrance.

At that moment, I couldn't help but wonder if any of the mischievous creatures were squashed beneath him during the chaotic descent. Despite the chaos, a part of me hoped that everyone present would emerge from this unharmed.

After all, this conflict wasn't really their burden to bear.

"I won't sit here talking all day!" Senán exclaimed. He attempted to goad Maelgwn into a trot, but there were too many púcaí surrounding them for him to move effectively. "It's time we made our point with a bit of combat. Quit being cowards and fight me like warriors!"

"Yeah, 'e's bang on," Eald grunted. "I used to fink I was a right numpty for takin' the easy way out, maybe I was a bloody coward back then. But I ain't bloody scared no more. I'll back up Sorcha whenever she needs me. So, let's dive in and sort this out once and for all."

I wasn't sure I found Sorcha deserving of such a lovely thought.

However, resisting the púcaí turned out to be quite challenging, especially when they refused to retaliate. It felt wrong to attack someone with a chair leg when their response was simply to accept it. Even Ruairidh, seemed taken aback by the situation. However, it was Senán who appeared to be the most deeply disturbed out of everyone in the room.

"Why are you here, if not to fight?" I yelled above the hubbub around me.

"Rígán wants you and only you at the castle, mate," the same púca explained. "Come with us and we'll let the rest off the hook. They're not involved in this and you know it."

"Sorcha, bide wi' me, dinnae gang awa', please!" Ruairidh pleaded pitifully, breaking my heart with his tone.

"I won't let you take 'er without a scrap, Dunstan," Eald objected. "You're well aware of that, ain't ya?"

"By my honor, there's no chance mo stór will be leaving with you." Senán vowed. "We'll defend her with our last breaths."

I found myself gripped with genuine fear as the possibility of that dreaded outcome loomed before me. The unfolding narrative had taken an unexpected turn, leaving me bewildered and unable to grasp the reasons behind it.

Under no circumstances would I allow those dear to me, nor Sorcha herself, to face death on my behalf.

"Everyone calm down," I begged. "No one needs to get hurt, especially not for me. You're all so brave and kind and wonderful, please let me save you any pain I can."

Senán and Eald both looked like they were about to protest some more. Then, Ruairidh started sobbing, his entire body shaking in grief. I couldn't stand it; his agony was too raw.

"Let Ruairidh come with me at least," I pleaded with Dunstan, who seemed to be in charge, my eyes filling with tears. "He won't be any trouble, I promise."

"Fine!" Dunstan relented. "His misery is too much for me as well. But the others gotta stay. And don't you dare 'ave any funny ideas, if anyone tries summat, we'll drag you back by force."

~ Rígán ~

I strutted around the throne room, bursting with pent-up energy and unable to wait patiently. I had been keeping a close eye on her safety for quite some time now, but I craved more. Giving in to obsessions was never a smart move; it always led to trouble.

But I couldn't resist indulging even the smallest of urges; it just wasn't in my nature. I nabbed my shillelagh[40], a grand bit o' kit with a flashy knob all sparkling with jewels.

Scrying weren't no fecking simple task without the right gear, but with my strong intentions and boundless energy, anything could be made possible. Bowing to my desires, the gem cast forth the very sight my heart longed to see.

She promptly materialized before me. I couldn't discern what was unfolding, but it was evident she was out of danger.

Mo bod stiffened as I witnessed her tear-stained countenance.

Ruairidh clasped her hand as she trailed Dunstan, completely encircled by púcaí. I wasn't certain why Ruairidh accompanied her, but it was of no importance.

In a mere few minutes, she'd be mine, she wouldn't bleeding escape me again.

I'd govern her joy and her suffering. The mere thought made mo bod swell even more.

I was well aware that it would take some time, and perchance many tears, but eventually, she'd relish being mine.

---

[40] Shillelagh (shi-lay-lee): A wooden walking stick with a large knob at the top that may be used as a club.

~ Moira ~

The torches illuminated the steep and seemingly never-ending stairs leading up to Rígán's castle. I could hardly consider them 'stairs' given their treacherous nature.

Occasionally, the pitter-patter of raindrops could be heard as a light drizzle began to fall, coating the pathway and adding a soft rhythm to our footsteps. The scent of damp earth filled the air, mingling with the earthy fragrance of fallen leaves and the subtle sweetness of blooming wildflowers.

With each step I took, my thighs burned and I couldn't help but curse Rígán for creating such an outrageously long pathway carved into the hill. Various explanations crossed my mind as to why these stairs were constructed in such a dumbass manner, but none of them offered any solace or made my arduous climb any more bearable.

The purgatory of the climb permitted me time to really think. I had no explanation for the why or how of anything since the Farmers Market. Pondering over those matters seemed futile, as it wouldn't lead me any closer to finding answers.

My understanding of 'An Cathair Ghríobháin', which seemed to hold some connection to the unfolding situation, had been partially useful in navigating this surreal realm.

The task of reuniting Ronan with his family had fallen upon me, and my only wish was for the real Sorcha to be waiting for him there. I didn't know how real this place was, but I wasn't going to let a baby, or anyone else, suffer because of me.

Rígán was both everything and nothing like I had imagined him. I felt drawn to him in a way I had never experienced before. However, if I wanted to accomplish anything, I had to set aside those thoughts and focus on the task at hand.

Regardless of my previous failures to prove I wasn't Sorcha, it seemed vital that I persuade Rígán to believe I wasn't her. Then I could focus on imploring him to help me find a way back home, preferably before I was run over by a godsdamn bus.

After what seemed like hours, though it was likely closer to half an hour, I finally reached the top of the hill and stood before the castle's portcullis. The flickering light of the lanterns and torches made the castle's intricate carvings and embellishments almost seem alive.

Startled, I leapt in surprise when the portcullis suddenly began to rise with a loud, metallic clanking. Shortly thereafter, the castle doors burst open with a thunderous boom, their echoes reverberating through the air.

"Oi, quit dawdling!" Dunstan grumbled, indicating he'd like us to enter the castle. "Rígán's expecting ya in there."

"I don't see Rígán," I idly mentioned, walking slowly into the castle entrance.

"Doesn't matter if you lay eyes on him or not, he's waitin' for ya, mate," he replied with a shrug.

What were we walking into?

I had all but forgotten that the last time I saw Rígán, I was involved in kicking him in the junk. Since then, my mind had been consumed with thoughts of the kiss, conveniently avoiding any other aspects of our interactions.

As I made my way through the entrance hall, a sense of anticipation filled me.

The grandeur of the castle's architecture hinted at the magnificence that awaited me within the castle. With each step, the atmosphere grew more captivating, and as I

reached the threshold of the next room, I beheld a sight that left me breathless.

The doors swung open, by themselves, revealing a scene that seemed to transcend reality. Candlelight danced, casting flickering shadows that played upon the walls adorned with intricate vines and blooming flowers.

But it was the centerpiece that truly commanded attention - the magnificent throne. Crafted from dark, contorted wood, its imposing presence seemed to draw me closer. Elaborate carvings of spirals and vines adorned its surface, a testament to the skilled craftsmanship that brought it to life. The seat itself, draped in opulent green velvet, shimmered with golden and silver threads skillfully embroidered upon it.

And there, above the throne, perched a raven-like púca, casting a foreboding shadow that loomed over the entire room.

Once we were in the throne room, it became evident that Rígán was, at the very least, not present. Maybe he was invisible or concealed somewhere, although it seemed peculiar for him to do so after compelling me to accompany him here. But in this world, you never knew for sure.

Rígán burst dramatically through another set of doors into the throne room.

I attempted to restrain myself from rolling my eyes at the spectacle, but I struggled to resist ogling him. His clothing was exquisitely tailored, accentuating every muscle and contour of his body.

"Cead mile failte,"[41] he crowed. "Tá áthas orm gur féidir linn aithne níos fearr a chur ar a chéile ar deireadh."[42]

"English, please," I reminded him softly.

"Oh, I see, I forgot that you only speak English," he sneered. "I was daft to think Sorcha was Irish. But you're not Sorcha, are you?"

I felt an overwhelming sense of excitement when he expressed his belief that I wasn't Sorcha.

---

[41] Welcome.
[42] I'm glad we can finally get to know each other better.

However, that feeling quickly dissipated as Ruairidh's high-pitched whine conveyed his distress, leaving everyone feeling tense and uneasy. He tightly gripped my hand and gave Rígán an intense glare, signaling that a chaotic and troublesome situation was about to unfold.

"Ruairidh, shut it! You're giving us all a fierce headache," Rígán grunted. "Teàrlag, show him the door and maybe give him a wee bribe to settle his jitters."

Teàrlag jumped down from their perch atop the throne and ambled over to us.

Ruairidh was having none of it and looked ready to fight to stay by my side. Teàrlag didn't seem opposed to that outcome.

"Quit yer bletherin' and dae as yer telt," Teàrlag fumed. "C'mon, ye overly touchy eejit, and I'll get ye somethin' tasty tae munch on. Mibbe I'll even let ye hang aboot wi' Roanan, the only other wee bairn here, fer a wee while."

"Ah'll nae gang wi' ye," Ruairidh snarled. "Ah jist want tae be wi' Sorcha."

I had little to no clue what they were saying, but I could tell Ruairidh wasn't about to leave my side.

"Make sure he's with Teàrlag," Rígán directed to me. "I won't put up with that kind of behavior, and I'd rather stay out of it."

"Ruairidh, everything is going to be alright," I cajoled as I gave him a big hug. It seemed wise to not escalate the situation and I didn't want Ruairidh getting hurt. "Could you do me the biggest favor and go with Teàrlag to check on

Ronan? I need to know that he's okay and that someone is there to keep him safe for me."

"Aye, ah reckon ah could gang check on the wee bairn Ronan," Ruairidh mumbled. "Ah'll keep him safe fer ye an' make sure ye get him back."

"Do you think maybe the other púcaí could leave too?" I asked while Ruairidh and Teàrlag left past Rígán. "I think it might be easier to talk if it's just us."

"Gach duine amach!"[43] he roared and the room quickly cleared.

---

[43] Everyone out!

Chapter Six

~ Rígán ~

With none but us two present, my desire for her was all-consuming. The fecking things I wanted to do to her were enough to make a saint blush. I saw no reason to wait any longer. It was just a matter of putting a collar on her and making her mine.

She was quivering like a leaf as I strutted up to her.

And the way she was eyeing me, I knew she was aching for it just as damn much as I was. Before long, she'd be nothing but pure bliss, having the honor of being with me. I casually swept a lock of her gorgeous ringlets from her face, and the way she melted into my touch let me know she was keenly aware of my every move.

Poor girl was looking a bit rough around the edges after all that mad dashing about and skirmishing. A good soak in the tub and some fresh rags would sort her shite out in no time, though.

"Uh…" She fairly cut across my thoughts and took a step away from me. "It seems like we have a lot to talk about…"

Feck's sake, what did she mean by that?

But sure, there was nothing more to say. She was mine, fair and square. The thirteenth hour was nigh, and Ronan was about to turn into a púca. All was grand and as it ought to be.

"It's a relief that you understand I'm not Sorcha," she continued on when I gave her nothing. Obviously, she had a bee in her bonnet. "My name's Moira. I'm not sure how I got here or why everyone thinks I'm Sorcha… Where I'm from, this is all a part of a story I've read dozens of times. Although, some things have definitely been different…"

It was a damn fact that no mortals hailed from Tír na nÓg.

The notion of her not being Sorcha did throw me off. And as for this all being part of some bleeding yarn, well that just added another layer of mystery to the mix. But I'd unravel this whole thing soon enough, make whoever's fecking responsible pay for messing with me, and then we'd have all the answers we needed.

But for now, before I exert any effort elsewhere, I just wanted to enjoy my prize.

"Take it handy, Moira," I drawled. "I've caught you, you're mine now, and I'll sort everything out. No need for you to fret yourself over anything."

I went to grab her hand, but settled for her wrist when she tried to dodge me. She looked fair spooked, mo bod throbbed and I had to admit, it gave me a bit of a thrill.

I wasn't exactly shocked that it wouldn't be easy to tame her, in fact, it pleased me a bit. She'd be a damn challenge, but I was up for it.

"I only belong to me! And you did not catch me! I agreed to come here," she seethed while flailing about, trying to wriggle free from my grasp to no avail. "I will kick you again if you don't let go."

She was pure dead cute when she made her threats, like a wee kitty bravely taking on the sun. Credit where it's due, last time she caught me unawares and it bleeding stung like the devil. I pondered whether I'd ever grow tired of her resistance, but somehow, I reckoned I'd always find it delightful and beguiling.

"Don't fret, I won't be underestimating you again," I teased her with a winsome grin. "But I do pray you keep pushing back. I've grown quite fecking fond of your spark, so do try never to lose it."

Her plush demeanor clashed with her scowl, and I cherished her all the more for it. It was evident she desired me, and I had yet to encounter another who enticed me as much as she did.

Clearly, I owed my profound gratitude and vicious retribution to whoever was meddling here. This had turned out to be a far more engaging few hours than I could have ever foreseen.

She tried to boot my shin, no doubt with some force, but I nimbly dodged it and used the chance to throw her off balance and draw her into my chest.

I seized the hair at the nape of her neck with a strong grip and wrapped my other arm around her waist, then crushed her lips with mine.

At first, she put up a struggle, but it wasn't long afore she surrendered to the flames of passion burning between us. She must've known, or at least sensed, as well as I, that our coming together was bound to happen. The connection between us was nearly touchable, far too real for anyone to disregard or deny for long.

I was a man consumed, with naught but the pleasure of her kiss on my mind. At the first chance, I intensified the embrace, my tongue plunging into her mouth to explore her depths.

Her moans were wicked, and I was uncertain how much longer I could contain myself to just kiss her. Both our breaths came in ragged gasps, filled with an ache of desire.

The air was positively charged with Boann's[44] arrival, and it took me a fair while to cop on, what with being so preoccupied with Moira. But sure, Boann being here only meant one thing. I held Moira tighter as I pulled away from her and cast my gaze over to Boann.

———————————————

[44] Boann (boh-an).

Boann was one Irish goddess who could turn heads with her great beauty. Her skin was as pure and white as freshly fallen snow, and her hair as black as a raven's wing. She was dressed in a flowing green gown that matched her eyes, adorned with necklaces, bracelets, and earrings made of the finest metals and gemstones.

Make no mistake, this lady was a creature of immense power and wisdom, with a bleeding razor-sharp wit and tongue to match. Boann, also known as the White Cow, was the one who created the mighty river Boyne, and ruled over the river of heaven, the great Milky Way.

And if you dared to cross her, well, you'd best watch out, for she wasn't one to be trifled with. Many a foolish soul met a quick demise for underestimating her power.

If I wanted this encounter to go well, I knew I had to treat her with the utmost respect and reverence. Boann was not just any goddess, after all, she was a great one, and deserved nothing less than the highest honor and respect. Now, having said all that, Boann and I tended to get along just grand, to be sure.

"Oh, my dear Rígán, there's truly no need to cling onto her so tightly," cooed Boann. "I assure you, I have no intention of pilfering her away from you, unless, of course, she has granted me her consent."

Sure, I let Moira go straight away, though it nearly killed me. There aren't many things that could make me give up my claim on Moira, but making it out alive after tangling with Boann was one of them.

I couldn't stand the distance that opened up between us as she stepped back, away from both Boann and myself.

"Is cuma liom ag iarraidh é a cheilt, thug mé anseo chugat í,"[45] Boann explained with a sly grin. "Her essence was adrift, and I could discern that she was your soulmate. You ought to be grateful that I was astute enough to perceive it and take action as I did."

Moira probably figured I'd gone and lost interest, or worse, didn't even notice her slipping out of the room. But it'd take more than Boann's entrance to make me miss a beat

---

[45] I am not trying to hide it, I brought her here to you.

in Moira's every move. Though, I can't deny that Boann had me captivated with her mere presence and what she had to say.

"Mar sin aithníonn tú í mar mo chuid féin freisin?"[46] I inquired of Boann in the most civil of tones.

"Indeed, my dear Rígán, she undoubtedly belongs to you alone, if that's the notion you're trying to convey," Boann chuckled. "However, I suspect that's not precisely what you mean by her being yours. Nevertheless, I wouldn't hesitate to retrieve her if she were to make such a request. It has been quite some time since the last pair of eternal lovers were unearthed, so you may not be aware, but there is a particular ritual you must undertake if you intend to be bound together until the end of time. And naturally, there is a price you must pay me for locating her and aiding you in keeping her."

"Cad atá i gceist agat a choinneáil?"[47] I inquired of her. I bleeding wished Boann would cease speaking English, there was no call for Moira to be privy to our discourse. "Tá sí agam cheana féin."[48]

The first toll of the thirteenth hour rang out.

I wasn't certain what Boann was at, but victory with Moira was nigh and Ronan would be mine to shape into a púca as I saw fit.

---

[46] So, you recognize her as mine too?
[47] What do you mean to keep?
[48] I already have her.

"Would it not be prudent to relocate this conversation to a realm beyond time?" Boann insisted, and transported us to one of her pocket dimensions. "Do not worry, my dear Rígán, for at times, surrendering a battle is necessary to triumph in the greater war."

As my throne room vanished from sight, the realm that greeted me was like stepping into a place that didn't belong to this world or any other I'd seen before. The air hung heavy with an otherworldly energy, crackling with the power of ancient times. It felt like time had taken a leave of absence, leaving us in a strange, timeless void.

Looking up, I saw a sky that stretched on forever, bathed in a twilight glow. The light it cast upon the ancient stones that surrounded us had a muted, mystical quality. Taking in my surroundings, I saw towering monoliths standing tall and proud, like sentinels guarding secrets untold. Their weathered surfaces bore carvings and symbols, holding mysteries from a distant past. The stones rose high from the ground, arranged in a circular pattern that stirred both awe and reverence deep within me.

The light that bathed this realm was something I had never beheld. Soft hues filled the air, lending an otherworldly glow to the ancient structures. Shadows danced upon the stones, creating an ever-changing tapestry of light and darkness, as if time itself played tricks within this enclosed space.

Amidst the wonderment, I couldn't help but wonder where Ronan was in this confusing place. Boann had brought him along, but his whereabouts remained a mystery amidst the enigma that surrounded us.

None of this augured well for me, and I was excessively fecking vexed with Boann's interference in my imminent triumph. I was bereft of any means to impede her, and in truth, I might have to offer gratitude to her against my will in the end, which only added to my frustration.

To overcome this and attain all that I desired was beginning to appear improbable.

My enchanting Moira was faring no better. Within seconds of our arrival, she had slumped to her knees. She had been unable to make her escape, not that it would have altered the situation even if she had, prior to Boann abducting her here. If I, with my resilience, found this dimension damn unsettling, it must be shattering her sanity.

"Rígán, ar mhaith leat a fhágáil anseo léi? Smaoinigh ar cad is fiú é, toisc go gcosnóidh sé go leor duit,"[49] Boann smirked like the cat that got the cream. "To be unequivocal, I do anticipate your assistance with mo mac óg[50], and I shall tolerate no excuses. Considering all I've done for you today, I believe it is a reasonable request."

Boann's desires would be fulfilled, regardless of my own fecking inclinations, that much was understood by both of us. However, for her to make such an offer, she must be seeking my complete devotion to the task at hand. Even if she acted as though it was not a request, and instead presented it as a proposition she knew I desired, it was clear that she had gone to great lengths to orchestrate this scheme.

Such comprehension was both captivating and unnerving.

"Moira, I can see that this is quite the burden for you, and for that, I do offer my sincerest apologies," Boann said as she extended a hand to help Moira up from the ground. She spoke with a calm and collected tone, though the weight of her words was not lost on anyone present. "However, the truth remains that you've been dealt a hand that must be played, regardless of your desires. Your mortal vessel has perished, and there's nothing any of us can do to alter that

---

[49] Rígán, do you want to leave here with her? Think about what it's worth, because it will cost you a lot.
[50] Mo mac óg (moh mah-ck ohg): My young son.

fact. Nevertheless, I have granted you a second chance at life as a Bean Sí when I discovered your spirit wandering aimlessly.

You may choose to remain with my dear Rígán, as I highly recommend, and if you do, certain arrangements will be made between the two of you. On the other hand, you may accompany me, and I will find a modest dwelling for you to establish yourself in. But let me caution you, if you select the latter, the journey ahead will not be an easy one. Tír na nÓg is not for the faint-hearted, and finding assistance without a cost will be a stroke of good fortune. Therefore, before you make a decision, ponder the matter with great care, Moira, as it shall determine the path your life shall take."

"Ah, Moira my dear, surely a life with me is far fecking better than being stranded and lifeless in bleeding Tír na nÓg," I drawled, hiding how it rankled me that Boann was giving Moira any choice other than being mine.

~ Moira ~

Shit had hit the fan so quickly I was reeling to keep up. Boann was not a character I knew from 'An Cathair

Ghríobháin'. In fact, nothing had been even remotely similar to the book since I arrived at Rígán's castle. I no longer had an idea what to expect.

I was devastated but not entirely surprised to hear Boann declare me dead and unable to return home. I had a million thoughts running through my mind, but Boann did not seem like the type to care about that and frankly she was terrifying.

The whole Bean Sí bit I would need more time, at a later date, to wrap my mind around. The most important question seemed to be whether I would choose a life with Rígán.

"Would I belong to him, like a pet?" I asked Boann.

"Indeed, I wouldn't underestimate my dear Rígán's inclination to undertake such scheming," Boann replied with a chuckle. "However, if you do decide to associate with him, it will be on equal terms. Nevertheless, I must caution you, it won't be without difficulties and challenges. Nonetheless, I can assure you, he won't subject you to any enduring afflictions."

"If I choose him," I speculated, "what are the promises that would be put in place and what would they do exactly?"

"My dear, what a truly captivating inquiry," Boann declared. "It strikes at the very core of the matter at hand. Through this handfasting, you will be bound to each other at the deepest level of your beings. Spare me the tedious questions about losing yourselves in the bond, for rest assured, you will remain yourselves in every meaningful way. Furthermore, each of you will be required to make a sacrifice of equal worth to demonstrate your unwavering devotion. This form of handfasting is far more enchanting and enduring than a mere marriage. The vows you exchange today will be unbreakable for all eternity."

Fuck me, this was serious. Worse, it wasn't all up to me. Rígán would have to be willing to make sacrifices as well.

Despite the profoundness of the moment, Ronan's giggles broke through the stillness. And there, in the distance, I caught sight of Ronan crawling about joyfully.

Why had she brought him here too? Why had she brought any of us here?

"Cén cineál íobairtí agus gealltanais a theastaíonn?"[51] Rígán all but snarled, clearly trying to keep his temper in check.

"Ah, finally, the beast shows its teeth," Boann said with a sly smile. "The offerings shall be of your own choosing, something that holds great value to you. And as for the vows, they will be binding and spoken sincerely. You will pledge to share everything for eternity, and be possessed by none other than each other. It is not a commitment to be taken lightly, but I trust that you both comprehend the gravity of the situation."

"Cén fáth a ndéanfainn an beart seo?"[52] he queried.

---

[51] What kind of sacrifices and commitments are required?
[52] Why would I take this action?

Boann sighed in exasperation. "Tá a fhios agam go bhfuil gach rud taobh istigh duit ag screadaíl chun í a shealbhú an t-am ar fad."[53]

"Sin go leor a thabhairt suas le húinéir uirthi,"[54] he protested.

"Listen carefully now, my dear Rígán, it's either you accept the deal or you don't," Boann grumbled, her annoyance palpable. "You must either find it worthy of your time or dismiss it entirely, but make no mistake, you shall still be assisting me with mo mac óg. Although, it will be considerably more challenging without her presence at your side. I am truly looking out for you both, so don't be taking me for a fool."

"Ah now, don't be getting cross with us," he said, trying to smooth things over. "We're just considering our options, aren't we, Moira?"

I knew there was a catch to all of this that I just couldn't see. More importantly, I knew Boann was not really giving me a choice. She made sure I'd have to be a fool to not choose Rígán.

My fate was sealed one way or the other, but maybe Ronan's wasn't.

"I'd be willing to choose Rígán if he's willing to release Ronan back to his biological family, as he found him," I stipulated.

---

[53] I know everything inside you is screaming to hold her all the time.
[54] That's a lot to give up to own her.

Rígán's nostrils flared at my offer and I was almost certain he would decline or at least negotiate. He paced and took deep breaths, trying to calm himself. It was more mature than I had thought him capable of being.

"Let me get this straight, I lose Ronan and pledge myself, all I have, for all time to someone I just met a few hours ago," he sneered, failing to be as respectful as he'd strove to be moments before. "And in return, I get the same, except all she has is herself, while I have a whole kingdom. Is that what you're offering?"

Boann's eyes went wide and I was sure she was about to do whatever goddesses did when someone pissed them off. "My dear Rígán, I beseech you to mind your tone. You are perilously close to testing my patience."

"Fine!" he declared much more civilly. "But if I'm parting with Ronan, I want her body, and I want it without any strings attached. Whenever and however, I want it. She has nothing else to offer me in exchange for him."

Chapter Seven

~ Moira ~

No way in hell I was agreeing to that. I wasn't so deep in denial that I couldn't admit to being wildly attracted to him, but that did not mean I was willing to give him my autonomy. I would figure out some way to live on my own, without these crazy supernatural assholes.

"Marvelous, indeed!" Boann cheered. "A bargain has been struck! Now I see your gob of protest, Moira, but I'd rather not listen to them, I must confess. So kindly keep silent, as my patience has been exhausted dealing with my dear Rígán. I won't release either of you from this agreement, regardless of your sentiments or thoughts. Now, I require both of you to hasten, as I am eager to leave, and clasp each other's right hands."

Rígán closed the gap between us and roughly grabbed my right hand with his. Strangely I noticed, in that moment, his hands were ever so soft.

I looked up into his determined eyes and knew there was no way out of this. I needed to keep my mouth shut or I'd make this infinitely worse for both of us.

Boann started chanting something and a blindingly bright cord of light began to weave itself like a snake around Rígán's arm heading towards mine.

My breath hitched, worried it would burn as it reached my hand, but it felt cool and silky. Then there was burning, it felt like my right wrist had been branded right over the pulse point. I held in my yelp of pain, not wanting to upset Boann further.

"Ah, it's all settled!" Boann boasted, much too proud of herself for my liking. "How fortunate that I happened to possess knowledge of the proper ritual."

The shining cord disappeared into our skin and I promptly pulled my hand away from Rígán.

The burning on my wrist had passed, but I could still see the brand it had left behind. It looked like two Celtic trinity knots,  flipped on their side and joined together to form one whole. I expected the skin to be red, swollen, and tender to the touch, but the burn already appeared to be perfectly healed.

Rígán grabbed my wrist to examine my brand and offered his in exchange. Asking would have been nice of him, but that seemed unimportant at the moment. His brand was similar to mine in that it was clearly made of two trinity knots, but on his darker skin it appeared almost white and reminded me of an owl swooping toward me.

"It symbolizes the preservation of individuality within each soul, encompassing the mind, body, and spirit," Boann offered. "However, the interweaving of the two knots to form a circle signifies an eternal unity between the two souls."

Great, I loved how everything here was done without my permission.

Not that I hated the brand, it was actually quite nice to look at. I just wanted my autonomy back; I had never felt so out of control of my situation.

"I shall make every effort to locate Ronan, even though it may disrupt his merriment, and ensure his safe return home," Boann explained as she began to disappear until it was just her voice left. "In fact, I shall take it upon myself to ensure the happiness and well-being of not only him, but also the true Sorcha and their entire clan. Consider it a wedding gift, dear Moira. As for you, my dear Rígán, I trust you have taken note of my benevolent intentions and shall keep them in mind for our next encounter. Rest assured; I shall pay you a visit in due time. You are free to depart with her whenever it suits you."

~ Rígán ~

I could sense Moira's very fecking being and feelings flowing through me. It was evident that we were far more intertwined than I had foreseen in this binding ritual. It was probable that she sensed my fury at losing Ronan and being compelled to comply with Boann's wishes. Additionally, I couldn't help but observe that after the damn bonding, I no longer found Boann as alluring as I once did, and my willingness to obey her commands - if they jeopardized Moira's safety - was now absent.

Moira was giving me the side-eye, a blend of prudence and bewilderment on her mug. Frankly, I wasn't in the mood to chat her ear off; I just wanted to grab what was mine and be done with this shite.

I planned on ensuring that the damn deal I was coerced into was to my liking. "Just one question, and then we'll head to my castle to sort out all my annoyances."

"Only one seems hardly fair and I'm not sure I'm in the mood for anything but figuring things out," she rebutted and her eyes became slits of vexation and incredulity.

"I could be arsed to not entertain any questions," I smirked, bonded or not, I held the reins.

She had to comprehend her standing in my realm. However, I couldn't fathom why I found her cheekiness so endearing.

She took a few deep drags of air while still glaring at me.

My temper was abating, and I was finding the scenario more amusing. Even more comical was that our chat appeared to be having the reverse effect on her sentiments.

"This is one question with a few parts," she announced, "What is a Bean Sí, what does that mean in relation to me, and how was being one of them affected by bonding with you?"

We both knew that was three queries, and I wasn't sure if I wanted to let her off the damn hook so quickly.

As much as I savored her annoyance, it'd be grand if she wasn't so fecked off. "Mo bhuanghrá[55], Bean Sí, they're the enchanting women of the Aes Sídhe[56]. Some refer to them as banshees, but it's entirely your choice if you fancy being a harbinger of death who wanders about wailing and lamenting. As for what it means for you, mostly that you've become a wee bit immortal, like the other feckers in Tír na nÓg. The strength of your intentions and energy will determine your power here.

Being locked to me with this ritual has loads of craic for you, but none of them alter your newfound status as a Bean Sí. For instance, you can probably feel my emotions now, if

---

[55] Mo bhuanghrá (moh wang-raw): My eternal love.
[56] Aes Sídhe (aysh shee-uh): The Irish term for a supernatural race of spirits known as fae in Celtic mythology.

they're powerful enough for you to bleeding catch on, but the bonding would've gifted you that skill whether you were a Bean Sí or a mortal."

I could see the gears turning in her noggin and sense her exasperation at not receiving responses to all her inquisitions. What a sharp-witted brain she possessed! I couldn't wait to tinker with it more. But for the moment, it was her body that I was eager to dominate and debauch.

I endeavored to disrupt her thought process as I made my way towards her.

I took hold of her and drew her close as I inclined my face towards hers. I sensed her bracing for a scrap until our lips locked and we both became lost in the deadly sensation.

Mo bod stiffened as I teased at her lips with my tongue and intensified the kiss as she yielded to me.

I whisked us out of Boann's freakish otherworld and into my boudoir.

The clock kept chiming thirteen as time reverted to its regular cadence. None of that mattered now, for I had only one thing on my mind and I wasn't gonna tolerate any more distractions.

I parted from her lips and yanked her onto my monstrous four-poster bed. She let out a gasp, and I sensed her astonishment and ire course through me, as she caught on that we were in my boudoir.

I used her momentary daze to latch onto the collar that had been lying on my bed and fix it snug around her neck.

The collar was a pure work of art, a masterful piece of wrought iron that was exquisitely crafted and intricately

designed. Its surface was etched with delicate filigree patterns that twisted and turned into mesmerizing shapes, with every curve and line melding perfectly into the next. But don't be fooled, it was more than just a pretty decoration; it was loaded with damn potent magic that severed one's connection to their own mystical abilities.

The choice of cold iron was a supreme act of caution, and I was grateful for it now. Not that Moira had a fecking clue how to tap into or wield her newfound stash of magic. Even if she was mortal, the collar was a powerful symbol of my dominion over her.

The sight of it on her neck was deeply enticing, mo bod continued to swell, especially coupled with the look of astonishment in her big, saucer-like eyes.

As I feasted my eyes upon Moira's face, I was eager to see her reaction to the grandeur that was my baroque-style boudoir. The room was oozing opulence and extravagance, with every bleeding detail meticulously crafted to my tastes.

The focal point of the room was the magnificent four-poster bed, adorned with plush, velvet fabric and golden tassels that swayed with each movement. Its sheer size could easily fit half a dozen gobshites, a clear testament to the excesses of my desires. But it wasn't just the bed that caught the eye; it was the iron chain, firmly fixed to the headboard, connecting to the collar now wrapped snuggly around Moira's delicate neck.

The walls were drenched in a deep red hue, enveloping the space in a passionate and lustful aura. Every inch of those walls was adorned with intricate carvings and gilded decorations, each stroke capturing the essence of opulence. Crystal chandeliers, lit by flickering candlelight, cast a warm and inviting glow, showcasing the ornate details with an ethereal shimmer.

I lifted my gaze towards the ceiling and feasted my eyes upon the majestic murals depicting fantastical creatures, their vibrant colors bringing the room to bloody life. Hovering high above us, they seemed to keep an eye on every move, whispering tales of power and desire.

Yet, as I eagerly awaited Moira's gaze to embrace the splendor surrounding us, I copped that her piercing stare was fixed on me, not the room itself. The shock in her eyes was mingled with a fiery anger and resentment towards my actions. At that very moment, it dawned on me that she probably saw this place as a damn gilded prison.

Though her reaction was a bit of a letdown, it mattered not a fecking jot. I knew she'd come to adore this room, especially since she'd be spending most of her time in it.

"What do you think you're doing?" she sputtered and pulled at the collar, trying fruitlessly to remove it.

I relieved her of her garments with a mere thought. The bond informed me of her mortification and unyielding anger.

Despite it all, she radiated brilliantly, without faltering, never attempting to cover herself or futilely trying to escape. She was a vision of flawless beauty, and I eagerly anticipated seeing her face, tear-stained and lost in pleasure.

"Ah, mo shíorghra[57]," I groaned, taking in her figure. "I crave you just like this, forever and a day. Now, hold steady, but fear not, for today I'll be a bit more tender with you. It's been a right tough ride for the pair of us."

Her mouth opened and closed like a fish out of water, but naught came out.

I suspected she wished to protest, but the magic would hold her to her vow. She would forever now always crave and desire what I offered her, whenever I wished it so.

~ Moira ~

I was alight in desire, physically unable to protest Rígán's advances, but mentally completely enraged and terrified by the situation. I wasn't embarrassed by my body's reaction to him, there wasn't a single moment I hadn't been turned on

---

[57] Mo shíorghra (moh heer-uh-grah): My eternal love.

by him, and I knew it was intensified by the magic of the bond.

I was incensed that I was chained to the bed and about to be taken without my consent. I wasn't able to force my body to move, it was all I could do to stop it from eagerly prostrating itself for his pleasure.

I was sure my body was releasing a heady cocktail of endorphins, dopamine, cortisol, serotonin, adrenaline, oxytocin, norepinephrine, and who knew what else into my system. On top of that, I could feel his ever-increasing arousal flowing through our bond.

I felt myself falling, no matter how hard I fought, into an almost trance-like state in which I could only recognize the aching need for his touch and approval.

"Taispeáin dom conas is maith leat teagmháil a dhéanamh leat féin chun súnás a thabhairt duit féin,[58]" he commanded and pushed me into a recline against the headboard. "Ná súnás gan mo chead."[59]

My body reacted immediately to his directions, somehow understanding him when I couldn't, and my mind floated along behind, too blissed out to care.

I relaxed into my favorite routine, already soaked in arousal, I swiped moisture up onto my clit and softly circled.

He leaned forward and pushed my knees further up and spread them open, watching intently.

---

[58] Show me how you like to touch yourself to give yourself pleasure.
[59] Do not orgasm without my permission.

His breathing became ragged and my heart raced.

I moaned and increased the speed and pressure as my clit began to swell, chasing my pleasure as he demanded. I would do anything to please him.

My core tightened, thighs beginning to shake, as my orgasm built.

He licked his lips, his gaze setting me even more aflame.

Gasping and keening, my circling tightened, and tensing I arched my back unconsciously pushing my breasts higher into the air and on display for him.

I was spiraling, my entire body shaking, right on the cusp of coming.

My fingers stopped, as he had ordered me to, just short of orgasm.

I sobbed in frustration, but knew I would always do what Rígán asked of me.

"Obair mhaith, mo bhuanghrá,"[60] Rígán sighed and my annoyance was replaced with euphoria, knowing my efforts had pleased him.

Rígán pulled me down the bed and crawled over top of me.

My hands were on him as soon as he was within reach, traveling up and down, desperately trying to pull the clothes from his body. I needed him to be as bare as I was.

---

[60] Good work, my love.

He smirked as he watched my frenzied attempts at divesting him of his attire.

His clothes were gone without a trace and I spared no thought for how, pushing my skin as close to his as I could. Pulling him on top of me, I wouldn't be happy until there was no space between us.

My legs circled his back and crushed my mouth to his, I could feel his equally immense desire.

I whimpered as he pulled away from me, placing his knees on either side of my hips, and comforting me with kisses down my jaw and neck.

He palmed my breasts, teasing and tweaking my nipples.

I moaned, trying to rub myself against him, as he continued sucking and nipping, working his way agonizingly slow down my body.

Rígán swirled his hot tongue around one of my nipples, sucking it into his mouth, still playing with the other, then alternating between them.

I panted and squirmed beneath him trying to get any type of friction where I needed it most.

He chuckled against my skin, amusement rolling off of him.

"Please, Rígán, please, please," I begged incoherently.

"Mo shíorghra, céard atá ag teastáil uait?"[61] he drawled, perfectly aware of what I wanted.

---

[61] My love, what do you want?

"Please let me come!" I begged shamelessly. "Please fuck me!"

"Fear not, mo bhuanghrá," he teased. "I'll take care of your desires at the right time. We've got a long journey ahead, mo shíorghrá, and I've got a load of plans in mind."

I whined, not happy with his answer, but unwilling to ever question him.

I ached for him, every part of me taunt and desirous of his touch.

But he knew what was best for us; of course, he would take care of me when it was right.

When I thought I might die from need, his finger briefly penetrated me, needlessly wetting my already slick clit, and leisurely circling. "Mo shíorghrá, you're absolutely fecking drenched, aren't you? Is this all because of me, by any chance?"

I keened and writhed, unable to form words to answer him. My only focus on trying to increase the pressure to where I needed it.

He was touching me just as I had shown him, but it wasn't nearly hard or fast enough to sate me and worse he knew it.

He continued to torture me as he kissed a path down my abdomen, scorching a trail of want as he went.

When his mouth finally reached my clit, I cried out in relief, and his fingers plunged deep into me, curling and pumping.

His tongue teased me and I bucked into his mouth, doing my best to fuck his face and fingers at the same time.

"Ná súnás gan mo chead,"[62] he pulled back to warn me again.

I wailed in irritation as another orgasm built, knowing I would once again be denied. Even knowing it was fruitless, I couldn't stop the coil of excitement twisting within me if I wanted to.

As promised, he stopped touching me the second I was about to come. I broke-down, crying in frustration.

"Obair mhaith, mo bhuanghrá,"[63] he murmured, soothing me. "I won't be holding you back any longer, mo shíorghra."

Rígán pulled my legs over his shoulders, mouth finding mine and I hooked my arms around his neck.

His cock slid through my folds, teasing my entrance, both of us moaning in anticipation.

He pushed inside of me in one thrust and I shrieked as my body stretched to accommodate his massive girth and length.

"Scíth a ligean agus tóg mé,"[64] he grunted, deepening our kiss.

My body complied and relaxed, letting him slide in further.

---

[62] Do not orgasm without my permission.
[63] Good work, my love.
[64] Relax and take me.

With his hands wrapped around my thighs and back, holding onto my shoulders, he continually withdrew and forced himself in farther.

I whimpered through the strain, sure he wasn't going to fit, but eager to please him.

He bellowed in satisfaction when he impaled himself to the hilt and his hips finally hit mine.

"Is this tickling your fancy, mo bhuanghrá?" he growled as he began to fuck me in earnest, hands hold my thighs in place.

"Oh gods, yes," I rasped, hormones already erasing the memory of the pain and replacing it with pleasure. My orgasm once again began to build, quickly tightening and twisting in my core. "I'm going to come!"

"Súnás domsa, mo shíorghra,"[65] he permitted.

I screamed as I climaxed, addled by the pulsing waves of euphoria, my body clenching around him.

He slowly fucked me through it, not caring that I was no longer present, lost in my own pleasure.

As I came back to myself, his pace picked up and became frenzied.

"I had a gut feeling you'd be into this, mo bhuanghrá," he groaned as he fucked me even harder, leaving bruises where he gripped me.

---

[65] Orgasm for me, my love.

His mouth found mine and he slammed into me several more times before coming inside of me.

He continued to kiss me, tongue as frantic as his pace had been, until he softened and pulled himself off of me.

Chapter Eight

~ Rígán ~

I was roused from my slumber by the sensation of Moira's wrath crashing into our connection. She was awash with indignation. At first, I feigned sleep, damn curious as to her next move.

I had kept her nestled in my embrace all night and now she was at last struggling to break free. Once she extricated herself from my embrace, she remained seated for some time, her gaze piercing through me.

I had almost resigned myself to slumber when she bleeding pounced.

Restricted by her collar, she was no more than a mortal, and her attempts at biting and scratching were akin to those of a kitten.

"Ah, go on and take it handy, mo bhuanghrá," I chortled as I took hold of her wrists. "You can't do me any harm, but it'd break my heart if you ended up hurting yourself with all this fuss."

"Now you fucking care about whether I'm hurt?" She seethed, gasping for air, consumed by her ire. She was truly exquisite. "You fucking raped me over and over again last night! I'm fucking covered in your bruises and bites! I can barely fucking move without feeling sore all over. I'm fucking chained to your godsdamned bed! Just… FUCK YOU!"

She was a damn sight to behold in her ire, all flames and fervor. Her countenance was aglow, her visage and bosom suffused with crimson, and her brow furrowed in the most charming fashion.

Mo bod swelled at the mere sight of her.

"Don't you fucking dare," She indicted me as she perceived the throbbing of my desire coursing through our bond. "I will never forgive you if you force me back under whatever it is that compels me to prioritize your happiness."

"Listen up, mo shíorghra, it was you who willingly got yourself tangled up in that vow and entered into that bleeding pact. I'm not the one pulling the strings or controlling the magic, alright?" I reassured her, although her words stung in the moment and the thought of her hating me was unbearable. "But here's the thing, if you were to fully surrender yourself to me without any reservations, the magic wouldn't mess with your personal experience. The enchantment only aims to bring forth what's necessary to fulfill your pleasure and desires, you get me?"

"You might not control the magic of whatever is going on, but you are fully aware of it!" She hurled her words at me like a blade.

Her tongue spoke true, yet I was growing damn vexed. Did she truly fecking believe that she would reap the benefits of our bargain without fulfilling her own end of the damn exchange?

"Ah, should I fecking ask Boann for a hand in fetching Ronan, then?" I scoffed. "To sort out the damn mess she caused last night, yeah? Having another púca by your side wouldn't hurt, mo bhuanghrá. I'm not particularly enthusiastic about giving up shite myself, mind you! I can't stand feeling your anger and hate pulsating through our bond. Ideally, I'd want everything to go my own fecking way. But that's not the case, and we both have to damn well adapt to the sacrifices we've made."

"I can't accept that! I wouldn't have made the deal if I knew what it would cost me." She was near to weeping, and her pain was becoming intolerable for me to disregard; I fecking despised the sensation of it churning within me.

"Hush now, mo shíorghra," I comforted her, enfolding her in a firm embrace and releasing the chain from her collar. "Sure, we've got eternity to get used to it, though I hope it happens fast as the wind. Let's freshen up, for everyone feels grand after a good scrub. Then we'll have a proper feast and I'll show you around your new abode."

~ Moira ~

I sullenly followed Rígán as he gripped my hand and walked through the castle. I could tell he didn't care for my lack of enthusiasm or admiration.

He prattled on incessantly, his voice filled with unwavering enthusiasm as he pointed out every minute detail of the castle that he held in such high regard. However, the intricate carvings on the walls, the elaborate tapestries that adorned every hallway, and the opulent chandeliers that hung from the ceilings were met with nothing more than my hollow gaze.

I didn't even bother to try to remember what he was saying or where anything was, I knew escape was impossible.

While I enjoyed feeling clean and he'd healed me, being groped while bathing and then fed, an admittedly decadent breakfast, wasn't going to make me change my mind about my situation. I wasn't naive enough to think being bonded to Rígán was going to be easy, without sacrifice, or allow me the autonomy my old life had; but I refused to just give away my basic rights because of some vow I'd been forced into.

For gods' sake, he fussed over my appearance like I was his doll, while he wore a variation of the same clothes as yesterday, and he refused to take off the symbolic collar he'd put on me the night before.

My captor styled my hair loose in soft ringlets and dressed me in a teal knee-length dress with a fitted bodice and billowing skirt. It was made of lightweight, shimmery fabric that reflected the light in shades of green and blue, the neckline was adorned with delicate copper embroidery, and the sleeves were sheer and fluttery. He paired it with knee-high boots made of supple leather, dyed to match the copper of the dress.

I looked enchanting and elegant; I would have loved it if I had chosen it myself.

"Whatever happened to Ruairidh, Eald, Senán, and Maelgwn?" I huffed, as the thought crossed my mind.

"Ah," Rígán faltered, taken aback by my random question after having not engaged with him since we left his bed. "Well, I'm not entirely sure. Ruairidh was kicked out of the castle last night with a satisfied belly and my assurance that you were doing well. Maybe he stumbled upon the others. I don't usually keep a bleeding close eye on each púca individually, if I can avoid it."

I didn't bother responding, he didn't deserve my courtesy or respect. All morning I had tried to push as many negative feelings through our bond at him as possible. I could tell it grated on him and hoped he'd choose to just leave me alone. So far, he wasn't rising to the bait, which made me even more irate.

"Considering you think the castle tour is pure bollocks, even though it's bleeding brilliant, I could bring you to the maze or city," he offered with a squeeze to my hand. "No need to argue; it could be a grand day spent in each other's company."

"The only way I'm having a delightful day is if you fuck right off," I snarled.

He shrugged, unaffected, and continued on with the tour.

I hated how sexy I still found him. I had to fight my instincts to stare at him and simper.

He was nothing like the Rígán I'd imagined all these years. Yes he was annoyingly as charming, handsome, and astute as I'd found him to be in the book. He was also possessive, unsympathetic, manipulative, and toxic as hell. Had he been that way in the book and I'd ignored it or were these dimensions of him that only existed in this reality?

Which parts of me truly found him so enticing that I wanted to forgive his every transgression against me and what part was the magic fooling me into feeling that way. Would it ultimately matter?

Either way, he was primed by his very existence and our bond to win this war of attrition. Until then, I was going to make him as miserable as I was.

~ Rígán ~

Ah, but the magic is a great thing altogether. It's all in the damn phrasing and intention, especially when someone else is handling it, but I learned that long ago.

Moira was already succumbing to the bond, but that wasn't surprising considering she's meant to love me to her very damn core, and vice versa. The magic just sped things up by allowing me to command her body to desire me whenever I saw fit.

Some might argue that the mind holds the reins over most matters, but one should never underestimate the sway one's internal systems and senses have over our perception of reality.

As much as it pained me to admit it, Boann may have done me a damn solid. If I had kept Ronan, I'd have thought I had it all for a while. But Moira would have been miserable, and that's not what I wanted.

Ah sure, she appeared quite wretched now, but I had a damn bit more sway in the matter than I would've had otherwise, and I'd endeavor to have her beaming in no time. I must admit, I found her attempts to convey her discontent rather diverting, and to be fecking honest, more captivating than she would likely care to know.

I had been restraining my emotions, hoping to allow her to vent and subside her temper, but the more she shot daggers at me, the more mo bod grew. It was beginning to feel as though her ire was a trifling cost to tend to my own desires.

"Why are you looking at me like that?" she snarled, evidently, I was divulging my cards without meaning to. "Stop making my body dump happiness inducing hormones into me. It fucking bullshit, I don't actually want you!"

Her passion was certainly alluring, but I'd sooner perish than hear her proclaim that she had no damn desire to be with me or had no love for me. No matter what she was spouting, my want for her was steadfast, and deep down, I knew the feeling was mutual. I may be ignorant of the mechanics of hormones, but I do know that magic can't compel someone to love another.

"Ah, don't you dare even think about mentioning the fecking notion of not wanting to be in my company or lacking any affection for me, you hear?" I rebuked her; she needed a lesson. "I appreciate your fecking passion and opposition, even your irritation and fear, but I won't stand for any fecking insinuation that you aren't completely mine in every bleeding possible way. If you keep persisting with such remarks, I'll have to find a much better use for your damn gob."

"I'm not your fucking possession!" she protested, indicating that the instruction I was imparting was not sinking in. "I don't want to be owned by anyone! I'm not yours to just play with! I don't fucking want you!"

"Ar do ghlúine,[66]" I commanded, pushing all my yearning through the bond. "Níl cead agat teagmháil a dhéanamh leat féin nó súnás."[67]

She whined and resisted, but as her gaze became unfocused, I fecking knew I had prevailed.

She descended onto her knees and gazed up at me with sheer admiration. This was the state in which I desired her to be, if only she could arrive there of her own volition.

"Open your gob and do me a favor.," I ordered, unleashing mo bod, already dreadfully rigid and dripping.

Moira ran her tongue along mo bod, sampling its flavor and gauging its girth in her mouth.

It was nigh too massive for her to accommodate in her gob, and she contended to take any fraction of it in.

Her proficiency and ardor were apparent, the sounds she produced were downright wicked, and it felt like pure bliss.

The intoxicating aroma of her desire wafted through the air, unmistakable and captivating.

"Do you enjoy making me feel this deadly?" I groaned, and her fervent nodding and cooing were all the answers I required.

Once I'd had my fill of her affectionate worship, I seized her head, keeping her firmly in position.

I fiercely drove myself to the hilt, reaching the depths of her throat and continuing to delve even deeper.

---

[66] On your knees.
[67] You are not allowed to touch yourself.

She choked on mo bod, but made a valiant effort to carry on and swallow it down.

The dread of being unable to breathe coursed through our connection, swiftly followed by the elation she felt from satisfying me.

"Relax, this won't fecking do you in," I comforted her, as I had no intention of ceasing. "Your earthly limitations don't matter now that you're a Bean Sí."

Tears cascaded down her visage as she gracefully acclimated herself to the situation, as best as she could, given the circumstances.

I thrust fiercely, savoring my own ecstasy, devoid of any apprehension for her.

Her bliss glided down our bond and elevated my mood as I persisted in employing her mouth.

I could scarcely discern anything through my groans, I was in raptures.

She drew me in to the utmost of her capability as I kept her immobile, drawing her cheeks as concave as possible, even when filled to capacity.

I clasped her head harshly against my frame and drove mo bod in harder, swifter, until I could no longer suppress myself, erupting in fervent spurts.

She consumed it all with enthusiasm and drew in a sharp breath as I extracted myself from her throat.

I caressed her visage with utmost regard, banishing the salty remnants of her sorrow. A vision of loveliness and perfection, she was. I dedicated a few moments to ensuring our appearances met the highest of standards.

It was unmistakable when she emerged from the enchantment her being and the sorcery had cast upon her. She was seething with fury and unfulfilled desires. I remained unapologetic, for it had been a fecking delightful experience, and a damn touch of retribution would ultimately serve her well.

~ Moira ~

I stormed blindly through the opulent hallways, my dress swirling around me with each angry step. The echoes of my own footsteps mingled with the pounding of my heart, drowning out the sounds of Rígán's heavy footsteps as he chased after me.

His voice, filled with anger and frustration, reverberated through the ornate corridors, amplifying my determination to get away from him, to escape the suffocating atmosphere of the castle that felt like a prison. As I sprinted, my mind consumed with the need to find an exit, I somehow found myself at the backside of the castle.

In my desperate haste, I flung open the nearest door, not bothering to check what lay beyond. The fresh air rushed in, a welcome relief from the stuffiness that had engulfed me for far too long. The door slammed shut behind me, cutting off Rígán's voice and sealing me in temporary seclusion.

Outside, the world seemed to open up before me. The sprawling castle grounds stretched out and the cool breeze caressed my flushed face, carrying with it a sense of liberation. It whispered promises of freedom and solace, urging me to keep running, to put as much distance as possible between myself and the source of my frustration.

I didn't stop until I reached the very edge of the castle grounds. Collapsing onto the grass, I gasped for air, my chest heaving with exhaustion. The weight of my emotions bore down on me, and I could feel the adrenaline slowly receding, leaving behind a mixture of anger and fear.

The castle loomed behind me, its imposing silhouette a constant reminder of the confinement I had momentarily escaped.

The rustling of leaves in the gentle breeze filled my ears, the distant chirping of birds, and the distant murmur of a nearby stream offered a soothing soundtrack to my turbulent thoughts. The scent of freshly cut grass and the subtle fragrance of wildflowers mingled in the air.

In that moment, beneath the open sky and away from the oppressive presence of Rígán, I felt a flicker of peace. It was a temporary respite, a stolen moment of tranquility before I would have to face the reality of my situation once again.

I knew he let me get away from him, but I was too relieved to have a moment to myself to think about why. I allowed myself to savor the freedom, to let the anger and fear gradually subside, and to gather the strength to confront whatever lay ahead. I was free to make my own choices, for a few moments at least, and I would do everything in my, admittedly limited, power to ensure I never had to return to that gilded prison again.

I sat up and took in the breathtaking view of the sprawling city and the surrounding forest below me. The morning sunlight bathed Púcaí City in a soft, golden glow, illuminating the once deserted streets that now bustled with life. The torches and lanterns that illuminated the city at night had been extinguished, replaced by the natural light.

The púcaí hurried along the streets going about their daily routines, each with their own purpose and destination. Some exchanged quick, cheerful greetings, while others engaged in animated discussions.

As my gaze wandered further, I caught sight of the forest that stretched beyond the city's edges. The emerald green canopy formed a serene backdrop, that enticed me much more than the bustling city.

And then there was an cathair ghríobháin, the sprawling maze that surrounded Púcaí City. Its twisting paths and towering hedges were a marvel of both natural and magical craftsmanship that seemed to stretch infinitely into the distance. From my vantage point, I could see the play of sunlight filtering through the leaves creating a dance of light and shadow. I imagined that if I listened hard enough, the

verdant foliage would whisper secrets about its concealed mysteries, hinting at the perils that awaited within.

I knew it wasn't just in my imagination that an unmistakable air of danger clung to the maze. The paths themselves were narrow, barely accommodating the passage of a single person at a time. They twisted and turned in a mesmerizing dance, entwining and diverging with bewildering complexity. It was an intricate web of possibilities, where wrong choices could lead to a never-ending loop, trapping wanderers within its maddening embrace.

I knew, from the book, that each area, like the cemetery, within an cathair ghríobháin had its own unique characteristics and allure, offering a diverse tapestry of experiences within the maze's complex design. And that amidst the tangled corridors, there were no guiding markers or distinguishing features to offer solace or direction, further heightening the sense of disorientation and vulnerability.

I couldn't help but marvel at its unfathomable intricacy. Maybe Sorcha's way into this mess would be the way I escaped from Rígán, out into Tír na nÓg.

Chapter Nine

~ Moira ~

I sprinted down the steep hill, my heart pounding as I fled Rígán, my feet struggled to find solid ground on the treacherous descent. The adrenaline coursing through my veins pushed me forward, propelling me with a reckless determination. I stumbled over rocks and brambles, falling several times, as I careened towards the city that lay ahead.

I was dirty and bleeding by the time I reached the city, but I couldn't let that slow me down.

Entering the bustling city, I maneuvered through the narrow streets, my senses on high alert. Colorful tapestries fluttered in the breeze, suspended between the wooden structures standing tall on stilts. The aroma of sizzling street food wafted through the air, intermingling with the scent of fresh blooms that adorned every corner.

Dodging startled púcaí, I weaved through the narrow streets, their wild forms darting in and out of my peripheral vision. Their mischievous grins and curious eyes followed my every move; their presence both exhilarating and unnerving.

Leaving the city behind, I entered the forest, my lungs burning with exertion.

The towering trees stretched towards the heavens, their branches reaching out like ancient guardians. The spindly trunks cast long, haunting shadows that danced across the forest floor. Sunlight filtered through the dense foliage, creating a patchwork of light and shadow that played hide-and-seek with my senses.

With each ragged breath, the scents of earth, moss, and decaying leaves filled my nostrils.

As an cathair ghríobháin came into view, my eyes were drawn to its unending hedges and promise of reprieve from Rígán. The thought of entering it willingly terrified me, but less so than the thought of submitting to the life that had been forced upon me.

Then, on the edge of the forest, a glimmer of unexpected beauty caught my attention. A lake, out of place amidst the wildness of the woods, shimmered in the dappled sunlight. It called to me, its tranquil surface offering a momentary respite from the chaos and intensity of my flight.

Veering off course, I made my way towards the water's edge, sinking to my knees as I reached the lake's embrace. Exhausted and breathless, the cool breeze brushing against my sweat-drenched face and enveloped me in the calming scent of fresh water.

The slowing of my rapid breaths hypnotically mingled with the gentle lapping of the lake's waters, quickly ushering my nervous system into a state of relaxation. I gazed out across the glass-like surface, mesmerized by the mirrored reflection of the sky above. For a long moment, I remained there, staring into the water as if lost in thought.

Though an cathair ghríobháin still lay ahead, beckoning me with its mystery and promise of escape, for now, at least, the world could wait.

My eyes were drawn to a single swan swimming gracefully on the water's surface. As the swan swam closer, I was struck by its peculiarities, that were maybe common here but odd to me; the swan's feathers were an almost glowing pristine white, and around its slender neck hung a delicate necklace made of gold and silver.

In the distance, I could hear a massive flock of birds making their way towards me, their wings beating rhythmically as they flew. As they drew near, I saw that they were also swans, their white feathers gleaming in the sunlight.

The veritable army of swans alighted gracefully near the solitary swan and around their necks swung a similar delicate necklace made of only silver. They moved with an elegance that seemed almost otherworldly, gliding across the water as if it were the most natural thing in the world.

Lost in thought, I sat there, watching the swans as they paddled about on the lake's surface, their necklaces glinting in the sunlight.

~ Rígán ~

Sure, there wasn't a single place Moira could leg it to that I wouldn't be able to sense her presence or find her without a hitch. I let her outrun me in the castle, giving her some space to calm down. I had other bits and bobs to sort out anyway.

When she left the damn castle grounds and Púcaí City, I was on top of all her moves. She fled towards an cathair ghríobháin, which was a right daft choice if you asked me. I had a good laugh thinking about how that played out.

Maybe the damn maze would teach her a lesson and she'd finally fecking appreciate what a great company I was.

151

Either way, I knew I could nab her the moment she got in trouble or I wanted her back.

Why she stopped at the damn lake was beyond me. I wondered what made her calm down after being so furious and determined. So much of what she did and said puzzled me, so why would this be any different?

"Dunstan, Teàrlag," I bellowed for my generals, who promptly appeared at my side. "Keep an eye on Moira and make sure she doesn't fecking end up in a right mess, yeah? One of you fill me in on what she's up to, if anything interesting goes down. If she gets fecking hurt or you fail to tell me something important, I'll hold the pair of you fecking responsible. And Teàrlag, don't bleeding cock it up again, alright??"

In just twenty-four hours, I had already changed myself to meet Moira's damn needs. I was speaking English more often than I'd like, even though I preferred Irish.

I knew she didn't see it that way and hadn't yet learned to appreciate all her time with me. But I knew she'd soon come to realize all I did for her, and that she was the only one, after living for a millennium, that I'd ever taken into consideration for the damn long haul.

~ Moira ~

Slowly I realized something was amiss. It wasn't natural for me to sit and contemplate nothing, tranquilly letting my chance of escape slip through my fingers. Something magical was happening and I wanted nothing to do with it.

I stood to leave and a swan left the flock and drifted towards me. As I watched, the swan with the gold and silver necklace began to transform before my eyes. Its feathers receded, replaced by smooth skin, and its long neck shortened, becoming that of a human.

In a matter of moments, the swan had become a beautiful woman.

She appeared to be in her twenties, with pale skin that seemed to glow, giving her a luminous and divine appearance. Her long black hair cascaded down her back in gentle waves, adding to her enchanting appearance. And around her slender neck, rested the same delicate gold and silver chain. She was wearing a flowing white dress, embroidered with intricate designs in gold and silver. Delicate depictions of swans adorned the fabric, their wings outstretched in flight.

I barely had a chance to wonder at who she might be, before she glided over the water's surface towards me and the shore.

Part of me knew I should leave, but I was drenched in a sense of serenity and felt no fear. I'd survived everything so far; this woman couldn't possibly be a threat to me.

She delicately stepped up onto the shore next to me and gave me a faint smile. She was a little shorter than me and very slender.

For some reason I really wanted to reach out and hug her, she just seemed so sad to me.

"Ah, begorrah, a most bewitching spectacle that meets me gaze this day," she said with a soft Irish accent. "Pray, do not inquire as to my identity, but never afore have I beheld the likes of you in these parts. I beseech you, reveal unto me, when did you become the latest possession of Rígán, that shadowy and inscrutable king of these lands?"

"Rígán does not own me," I protested, still too relaxed for there to be much fire in my words. "He might believe otherwise, but I only belong to me."

"Ah, begorrah, and it's a fairly recent acquisition, ain't it?" she mused. "Seldom does he cast his gaze upon companions with such fondness, hence you must possess an enchantment of your own. The gentleman remains a riddle, yet I discern a glimmer of genuineness in the depths of his affection for you."

"Regardless, his affections and needs are not the only ones that matter," I objected with an eye roll. "I was promised an equal partner, not subjugation."

"Ah, now, it's a rare occurrence to stumble upon such a progressive notion as an equal comrade in these parts," she began, eying my collar. "It runs contrary to the ancient customs, where might dictated right and strength reigned supreme. In the realm of Tír na nÓg, power and dominion hold the key to one's fate, and equality remains a whimsical fantasy. Aye, it's a mysterious thing, this notion of equal partnership. It challenges the very fabric of our society, and those who embrace it are often regarded with suspicion and mistrust. But perhaps there's more to it than meets the eye, and maybe, just maybe, it's a concept worth exploring further."

"You sound like you're talking from personal experience," I ventured.

"Ah, my dear friend, maybe it could be so," she said with a smirk. "But, in all honesty, I'm intrigued to glean your contemporary ruminations on the subject. Would you mind taking a seat with me for a spell and indulging in a chat, if it's not an undue burden? There's a certain enigmatic ambiance wafting through the air today, and I find myself in the mood for a bit of discourse to while away the hours."

With a thought she called forth a wicker basket, seemingly out of thin air. It was filled with all manner of delectable treats, each one more tempting than the last. Next to it sat a bottle of champagne, and with a gentle pop, the cork flew off and the bubbly liquid poured into two delicate crystal flutes.

She then produced a soft, fluffy blanket, and spread it out on the grassy meadow.

Nothing in me rebelled from eating and talking with her, she seemed friendly enough and making friends might be the most helpful thing I could do at the moment. I followed her lead and relaxed onto the blanket with her.

She was kind enough to share the champagne and make us both plates of creamy cheeses, plump grapes, buttery croissants, cherry tomatoes, and tender spears of asparagus.

For a few moments we just sat and sipped champagne and nibbled from our plates. It was a companionable silence and I felt completely at ease. Soon enough, she seemed ready to share more than her company and food.

"Ah, the hushed murmurs of the Aes Sídhe bear truth, my dear friend. I am a daughter of the Túatha Dé Danann," she began her story. "In days gone by, I underwent a mystical metamorphosis from swan to maiden during Samhain, when the veil betwixt the realms of the living and the departed is at its thinnest. My power was great, surpassing even that of my father, yet I knew that one day I would be bound by the laws of our kind and compelled to wed a suitor selected by others.

Yet my spirit yearned for more. I craved the power to choose my own destiny, and with it, the freedom to select my own consort. And so, I cast my gaze upon a certain Túatha Dé Danann, whom I deemed to be the most fitting match. He was renowned for his honor, esteeming women greatly, and possessed the strength to safeguard me from those who sought to possess me. And so, I took matters into my own hands, and seduced him by visiting him in his dreams each night for a year, playing sweet music on my timpan. It was a daring and provocative act in those times, but I knew it was the sole means to win his heart.

When his kin discovered me, they demanded that my father grant my hand in marriage to my dream beau. Yet my sagacious father, aware of his limits, refused to grant that which lay beyond his dominion. He told my suitor that I governed my own life, and the only way he could earn my hand was to recognize me amongst my flock of swans, and call to me when I transformed on Samhain.

And so, it came to pass on that momentous night, my beloved journeyed to Loch Bél Dracon, the lake where I dwelt, and identified me amongst my swan companions. He called out to me, and I swam to him, revealing my human form. He beseeched me to be his wife, and I consented, on the condition that I retain the liberty to return to the water at my whim. And so, we swam as one, singing a dulcet melody that caused the townspeople to slumber for three days. It was a time of enchantment and amazement, a moment that will be forever etched in the chronicles of our people."

"Wow," I breathed in awe. Also, who or what were the Túatha Dé Danann? "That's amazing. It sounds like everything worked out the way you wanted…"

"Ah, my dear friend, indeed it is true that once upon a time, I did feel the same way," she explained. "At the onset of our love, it was so intense and all-consuming that I did not feel the desire to shift and frisk about with my swan companions. However, as the sands of time flowed, the yearning to transform and join them burgeoned within me akin to an incessant itch beneath my very skin. Nevertheless, my beloved persuaded me to remain steadfastly at his side, and I found myself powerless to resist his adoration and unwavering loyalty. It was quite delightful to be cherished in such a manner.

As the years flew by, the call to be free, to soar and swim and revel in my untamed nature, grew ever more commanding and unrelenting. I realized that I had been neglecting that part of myself for far too long, and I knew I had to answer the summons. Yet, my beloved was wounded by my yearning to spend time apart, and I endeavored to stay and bestow upon him what he required. Alas, the call to be whole and liberated was simply too potent, and I could no longer endure it. I absconded, seeking solace amidst the boundless heavens and invigorating, crystalline waters, taking the form of my swan self.

Now, I must be true to my authentic self, and if my beloved cannot embrace such verity, then I must embark upon a sojourn to ponder what this portends for us. Millennia are a long time, my dear friend, and relationships can be intricate and ever-evolving. Nevertheless, when the twilight descends, we must remain devoted to our innermost selves and obey our hearts, regardless of the paths we may traverse."

"That's a lot," I conceded, not sure what advice she thought I could give to help her.

I couldn't even conceive of being over a thousand years old. Let alone being married to someone for that long.

"Ah, it's said that Rígán is a generous lover, but it seems you've not lingered long in his embrace," she stated. "We find ourselves in akin circumstances, my dear friend, do we not? The enigmas of love can bewitch and bemuse in equal measure, and it seems we have much to deliberate. I implore you, do tarry awhile and impart your musings with me."

"Well," I began and thought I should be embarrassed at the direction of the conversation, but felt the need to be completely honest with her. "It's not that he isn't able to satisfy me per se, that isn't the issue at all, it's that he doesn't take my needs or wants into consideration at all. Boann bound us together in some sort of soulmate ceremony, now I can feel his strong emotions whenever they occur, and as part of the ritual we each chose something the other would sacrifice. Now, whenever he feels like it his carnal needs preempt my own and I completely become his plaything with no control over my own responses or desires. Does he make sure it's enjoyable for me? I guess, well yes, but I think that is just as much the magic of the situation ensuring I submit willingly to him. I just can't accept that."

"Ah, I do perceive," she reflected. "It is a most peculiar occurrence, my dear friend, for in these modern times, it appears that the fairer sex hath been endowed with greater autonomy in such affairs. It is a curious thing indeed, to hear of one who shuns the coveted mantle of soulmate, a rare and cherished title bestowed by a potent and generous gentleman. I myself have but lately come to the realization that I must assert my own independence, despite my lifelong devotion to the notion of carving out one's own destiny. Thus, I do comprehend your defiance of the bond, and I extend to you my deepest sympathies in your plight."

"Honestly, it's been a shit day or so for me," I disclosed, thinking back on recent events. "Not that I would ever be alright with just giving myself entirely over to someone else, but there is just so much for me to process. But on top of all that, I lost my life, as I knew it, career, and friendships. I've been mistaken for someone else and had to play along in a story that I wasn't meant to be a part of. I've done my best to make good decisions along the way, but it doesn't seem like I have control over the outcome of anything here. I feel completely out of my element and powerless. I hate it."

"Ah, pray forgive me, for I must confess that I am utterly confounded by your tale," she admitted. "Nevertheless, my dear friend, it does not escape me that if Boann herself was involved, then surely many aspects of the situation were beyond your grasp."

Chapter Ten

~ Rígán ~

"Cor, when we rocked up, she was already having a natter with the Young Son's Yew Berry, blabbering on about how much she misses her mates, Baz and Lex," Dunstan imparted, as I paced the throne room. "Sommat to do with being a brief-barrister, and how she was itching for a new gig to get her gnashers into. Mostly moaning about being a bleeding pushover and babbling about owning her own desires."

I mulled over Dunstan's blabber. The lad was known for his candor, but he was hardly an expert on the matter at hand. While the bulk of the intel wasn't novel to me, the fact that she was cozying up to a damn Túatha Dé Danann gave me pause.

Now, I'm not one to be easily rattled - little can perturb me. But those damn gods and goddesses are a whole different ball game. Best to steer clear of them and their machinations. And with Boann already in the mix, things were sticky enough. This was a complex web that Teàrlag and Dunstan were ill-equipped to navigate.

I focused my will, honing in on Moira's whereabouts, and behold, there she was, all alone.

A half-eaten spread and an empty champagne bottle were evidence of a recent indulgence. The lake still stirred with the wake of the swans that had since departed. The goddess was fecking kidding herself if she thought I wasn't privy to her sneaking about in my realm.

But right now, it wasn't my place to intervene, even though Boann was clearly gearing up to drag me into her damn schemes. I knew time was of the essence, though - I only had a narrow window before I'd be forced to take action, and risk both myself and Moira in the process.

"Finished prattling with the Yew Berry, I see?" I drawled, causing Moira to jump at the sound of my voice. "Personally, I'm rather bleeding curious about these damn Baz and Lex fellas you're fecking pining for. Do tell."

With a flicker of annoyance, she gave me the side-eye and let out a snort of derision. Standing, she brushed the crumbs from her skirt and began to stroll away.

I caught up to her in a damn hurry and clasped her wrist firmly.

"Don't be daft, mo bhuanghrá, thinking my words are just a suggestion." I hissed through gritted teeth, gutted that she could even consider other blokes.

I'll admit that I'd never hold her damn past against her. That would be pure bollocks, and I'd fecking burst out laughing if she ever attempted to do the same to me. But that was then, and this was now. She was mine, and I wouldn't suffer her yearning for anyone else.

"Spying on me?" she taunted, without a bleeding care in the world that I was in a fecking tizzy over it. "Not that it's any of your business, but Baz and Lex are just friends. Friends that are deeply and committedly in love with each other. In fact, I wish I had a relationship as respectful and thoughtful as theirs!"

"Oh, mo shíorghra, my love for you is fecking absolute," I retorted in a tone of refined disdain, defending my damn actions with conviction. "Honestly, you'll soon realize that thoughts of you never leave my mind. I couldn't be more fecking obsessed with you, if I tried."

"You know that's not what I meant," she snarled and made a frantic attempt to wriggle out of my grip.

I drew her near, encircling her with a firm embrace. As always, she strained against me, determined to break free from my grip. It was clear she had yet to learn the hopelessness of her struggles.

I leaned in, angling my face towards hers, and our lips met. The sensation was dizzying, my mind adrift in a sea of sensation. My lips moved over hers, savoring every moment of the electric connection between us.

My kisses were deliberate and unhurried as I drew her closer, my hands gripping her waist possessively.

At first, there was resistance in her body, but soon enough she gave in. Her supple form yielded to my touch, her softness filling my hands.

I was consumed by a primal desire that could not be ignored.

My kisses grew more urgent, my tongue exploring her mouth with an intense hunger that spoke to the passion that lay ahead.

With a low moan, I shifted my hand to the nape of her neck, deepening our kiss with each passing moment.

I sensed her needs aligning with my own, and I knew that we were both powerless to resist the intense pull that bound us together.

~ Moira ~

I was once again Rígán's to be used as he saw fit. Nothing mattered but being with and pleasing him. Every touch he gifted me, every sound of pleasure he made, fueled my arousal.

My nipples hardened, my core heated, and I was slick with desire. Only he could give me what I needed.

"Tell me you fecking want me, that you will be mine like this forever," he broke our embrace to demand.

"You're everything I want and need," I insisted, desperate for him to be happy with me. "No one will ever matter to me, but you. Tell me what you need and I'll do it."

"Ah, now, spill the beans - what craic did you have with the Young Son's Yew Berry?" he probed as he nipped at my earlobe.

"What?" I sighed, unable to fully focus on his question. "I only spoke with a swan lady today."

165

"Swan lady, is it?" he purred against my skin and kissed down my neck. "Go on, spill the damn tea about what she said about herself."

"Not much," I hedged, unwilling to part with her confidence. More desire pulsed through our bond and I felt faint from its onslaught. "She's having trouble with her husband respecting her wishes."

"Ah, I see," he whispered into my ear and sucked at my neck's pulse point. "And what was it she was after from your lovely self, if I may ask?"

"I'm not really sure," I admitted between gasps. "I think she just wanted someone to understand what she was going through. Maybe a friend."

Rígán hummed his acknowledgment but kept any further thoughts to himself.

His kisses trailed down my throat towards my breasts.

When he got to the neckline of my dress, he gently tore it entirely off my body, like it was made of crepe paper. I was left in nothing but the nude, lace lingerie and boots he had chosen for me earlier in the day.

He was still fully clothed, his erection straining painfully against his pants. I wanted us both to be naked as quickly as possible. I started taking off my bra and he stopped me.

"Mo bhuanghrá, you're an absolute fecking stunner," he groaned as he took me in. "Every time I lay eyes on you, I find myself more and more captivated by your charms."

I reached for him, intently tugging at his clothes.

He snickered, clearly amused with my impatience.

He stilled my hands and drew my face up to look longingly into my eyes.

"Sure, this is the way it's meant to be, and in no time at all, you'll embrace it willingly," he assured me.

"Yes, yes, yes," I chanted in complete agreement. "Please fuck me Rígán, I need you."

"Ah, go on now, plop yourself down on the blanket, mo shíorghrá." he requested, his voice dripping with desire.

I scrambled to the blanket, eager to comply. I laid down, knees parted, and propped myself up on my elbows. My only focus on moving things along.

"Tá do mionbhrístíní chomh fliuch is féidir liom a fheiceáil beagnach tríothu,"[68] he drawled and prowled towards me.

He kneeled in front of me, quietly focusing on where he could see my nipples poking through the fabric of my bra and arousal soaking my hipsters. A thrill ran through me, loving his rapt attention being only on me.

I wiggled trying to find friction and relief from the throbbing in my core.

"Ná súnás gan cead,"[69] he warned me. "Is liomsa amháin do phléisiúr."[70]

"Please touch me," I whined, but instinctively stopped moving, giving control of my pleasure to him alone.

---

[68] Your panties are so wet I can almost see through them.
[69] Do not orgasm without permission.
[70] Your pleasure is mine alone.

"Such a fecking good girl, mo bhuanghrá," he crooned. "No need to fret, for I'll be looking after your every whim and craving. Tell me, how head over heels are you for me, and how much do you rely on me?"

"You're my soulmate, my only and deepest love," I babbled honestly, saying the first things that came to mind. "You're so handsome and kind and strong and brilliant and wonderful, I want you every time I see you. You're all I can ever think about, you're my everything."

"Your words hit the spot, mo shíorghrá, and to hear them from your sweet lips is nothing short of pure bliss." Rígán smiled lovingly. "You are everything to me, whether you're burning with a deadly fire and talking tough, or soaked in want and shouting my name like a damn thunderstorm."

He teasingly ran his fingers along my soaked hipsters and I pushed up into him, attempting to deepen the contact.

I was on the verge of begging him again when he vanished them from my body, easily slipping two fingers into me.

I clenched, grinding into him, trying to give my body what it desperately wanted without breaking his rules.

He crooked his fingers, my moans and gasps spurring him on, and pumped into the spot I loved.

I whimpered, trying to make him pick up speed, but he just smirked and kept his pace agonizingly slow.

He grazed the thumb of his other hand against my clit and I cried out his name, bucking into it.

Too slowly he leaned forward, and lapped up my essence, watching my reaction.

"OMG, yessssss," I gasped and arched against his mouth. "Please keep doing that."

He gently began sucking my clit, curling his tongue in response to its quivers.

My entire body began to clench and spasm in response. I was close to coming and I didn't know how to stop myself.

"I'm going to come," I rasped, unable to not tell him.

"Ná coinnigh siar, mo bhuanghrá,"[71] he confirmed with a grin.

Pleasure burned through my system, short circuiting my brain.

I fell back, no longer able to hold myself up on my elbows, panting.

All the while he drew out every ounce of bliss my body could give.

"Ah now, fecking steady on there, take a few deep breaths," he teased. "We're far from the finish line just yet."

I did what he desired, I always would.

My breathing calmed and I became eager to continue. "I'm ready."

Rígán stood and vanished his clothing.

---

[71] Don't hold back, my love.

This was the first time I was really able to study his completely naked form. He stood tall, a towering presence, with a physique that was nothing short of awe-inspiring.

Every inch of his body was chiseled and defined, his muscles rippling under his taut, bronzed brown skin. His jawline, accentuated by the well-maintained stubble, commanded attention. The playfulness in his golden eyes hinted at the mischievous nature that lay beneath his handsome exterior. Yet the intensity of his gaze never failed to make my heart skip a beat. Every inch of his face, from the sensual lips to the angled eyebrows, was perfectly crafted, creating a masterpiece of masculine beauty.

His imposing horns, curving majestically from his head, gave him an air of wildness and strength that was both intimidating and alluring. His hair, thick and wavy, cascading down his shoulders in ebony waves, with just the tips of his pointed ears showing.

His broad chest and shoulders were a testament to his strength, and his powerful arms that I knew from experience could pick me up like I was a mere child. His abdomen was a masterpiece of sculpted perfection, glistening in the sunlight. The V-shaped lines of his hips led down to legs that were like tree trunks, muscular and powerful, with calves that flexed with every movement.

His tail flicked impatiently, catching my attention momentarily, until he began pumping the length of his already swollen cock until it was erect.

My heart raced at the sight of it. I knew it was large, but every time I saw it, I had to readjust to just how massive it was. There was such a thing as too big and he had more than crossed that line.

He lowered himself over me, kneeling on the outsides of my ribcage. His cock lay across my ribcage, breasts, and clavicle.

His fingers pinched and rolled my nipples through my bra, my breathing became ragged once again.

"Bain úsáid as do bhéal agus breasts chun mé a shásamh,"[72] he demanded and vanished my bra.

I pushed my breasts around him, fully encasing the girth of his cock.

Leaning my head forward I took the tip into my mouth, sucking and swirling it with my tongue.

Rígán growled and began to roughly fuck my breasts and mouth.

My spit slickened everything, making it easier for him to thrust in and out.

I focus on breathing and making him bellow in ecstasy.

"Ah, that's it, mo shíorghrá, you're such a good girl," he praised me as he came. "Swallow every last drop like a champ."

I took several deep breaths, a bit dizzy and exhausted from working his length.

He caressed my face affectionately, leaning down to kiss me.

---

[72] Use your mouth and breasts to please me.

I greedily ran my fingers through his hair and deepened the kiss, always wanting more of him.

"Smeach anonn agus greamaigh do thóin san aer,"[73] he commanded as he broke the kiss.

He rolled off me so I could flip onto my stomach and present myself to him.

I felt him move behind me and grab my hips, positioning me just the way he wanted.

I groaned as he kneaded my ass and my core heats and tightens with need.

He kissed the curve of my back and worked his way down, licking and nipping.

His tongue plunged into me, lapping and twirling, until I'm writhing in pleasure, panting, my fingers clenching the blanket.

I moaned as his thumb circled and teased lightly against the pucker of my anus. Some sort of magic was used to keep his fingers perfectly lubricated and it was absolute bliss.

"Listen here now, I want you to súnáis as often as you can, and don't you dare slow down until I give you the damn signal to ease up," he ordered me as he slid two of his fingers into my aching core.

I gladly obeyed, reaching up to stroke my clit just the way I needed.

---

[73] Flip over and stick your ass in the air.

I quickly came and he continued to pump his fingers into me languidly as I rode out my second climax.

Then he pushed his thumb into my ass, working more diligently to bring me to climax again.

"Coinnigh chuimil tú féin, ba mhaith liom súnás a thabhairt duit arís go tapa,"[74] he growled.

I began to gently touch myself again, I was still sensitive from having just come.

I whimpered as we worked my way quickly to another orgasm.

Rígán used one of his slicked fingers to penetrate my ass, I pushed back into it, relishing the additional sensation.

He continued to use both hands to push in and out of me, overwhelming my senses.

I mindlessly moaned and chanted his name.

I felt my core tightening and explode before I even had a chance to touch myself again.

He kissed my back as I twitched through the aftershocks of my fourth orgasm.

"Ah, my sweet one, you're doing fecking brilliantly," he murmured while adding another drenched finger to my ass. "Keep it up, mo bhuanghrá. One more for luck before we move on."

My clit was still overstimulated, I slid my fingers around its edges, not quite touching it.

---

[74] Keep rubbing yourself, I want to you to orgasm again quickly.

Grinding into Rígán's fingers as he fucked me, pumping and stretching.

I was already close to coming when he added a third finger into my ass, while still deliciously stroking my core.

I shattered, shuddering and crying.

"I can't," I gasped through my sobs, "take anymore. It's too much."

"I daresay you've got one more in you, but this time I'll let you off the damn hook," he promised, rubbing my back. "You just lay back and let me take control. Try to unwind as best you can, won't you?"

Hormones flooded my system and I whined my concession.

The head of his too fucking big, lubricated cock prodded and pushed into my ass.

He continued to slowly thrust in and out as I wailed, my body forced to adjust him even after all of the prep.

"Hush now, no need to shed tears," he rasped, still rubbing my back. "Just fecking bear down or loosen up, whichever brings you more ease."

I felt like I was floating as my body released a heady cocktail of euphoria into my system.

The pain was no longer an issue, moaning, I began to buck and grind into him, chasing my own pleasure.

He held my hips so he could continue to force himself in slowly, making sure to not hurt me more than necessary.

I gasped as he bottomed out and began to fuck me harder; I met each of his thrusts.

The feeling of fullness, wet sounds of his thrusts, and sensation of his balls hitting me just right was more erotic than anything I had ever experienced before.

I desperately wanted to touch my clit but it was still too tender.

Rígán grabbed me around the waist and pulled me onto his lap.

He tweaked and played with my nipples, kissing my neck, while I adjusted to the new position.

After a few moments, I reached around and grabbed on to his hips, using them to leverage myself as much as I could up and down his cock.

One of his heads left my breasts and he pumped his fingers into my core, being careful to not touch my clit.

"Listen here, mo bhuanghrá," he whispered into my ear. "You're fecking mine, every bleeding inch of you. I've staked my claim, and there's no going back. You're fecking mine, through and through."

"OMG yes!" I keened, completely lost to my own pleasure. "I only ever want to be yours. I love you!"

He pushed hard into the bundle of nerves right behind my clit and I howled, trembling violently as I climaxed.

Only barely aware of him grabbing my hips to thrust violently into me several times before coming.

He cradled me against him, my body too limp and muscles too exhausted to hold myself up any longer.

Chapter Eleven

~ Rígán ~

I was gobsmacked, watching my stunning Moira's bosom heave and fall, snug as a bug in my arms. Holding her like that was worth moving mountains for. She was the full package, she was. Smart as a whip, sharp as a tack, kind as a saint, and tough as nails. She'd argue with the best of them, but that's what made her so irresistible. Her drive and confidence were just what I needed in a partner.

I had to mind her, those damn Túatha Dé Danann feckers were way too interested in her. I could handle myself and the púca around them, but the thought of any harm coming her way made my blood boil. I'd burn the whole world down and sell my damn soul to keep her safe and sound, no question. That's just how it was. I'd do whatever it took to keep the púca and my shite in order, but not at her expense, no fecking way.

I brought us back to my, ah no, our boudoir. I grinned at the notion of sharing a bedchamber with her. She brought me pure joy. It's not my usual style to get attached so quick or to be so daft about someone, but love and soul bonding, they were fecking magnificent, I tell you.

If I hid her away for a bit, kept her out of everyone else's sight, maybe I could sort everything out on my own. She'd probably be fit to burst with anger at me, but I'd rather spend eternity making her forget and forgive my misdeeds than put her in harm's way, ever. She was already in a fierce rage with me for matters that I'm certain she'd come to adore, so what's a bit more ire?

I could make the room perfect for her, make sure it had every damn comfort and amusement imaginable for when I wasn't around to entertain her. What's a few years, maybe a couple decades at most, to immortals?

With my head screwed on, I got down to business. As she kipped away, I sorted out any niggles or discomforts she had and tidied us up proper, making sure we looked the part.

I fixed her collar on the bed, knowing full bleeding well the explosion of anger that would come when she woke. But it was a damn necessary evil.

I spruced up the room a bit, adding a few odds and ends I thought she'd fancy. I'd polish it up to her liking once I get the scoop on her tastes.

Chucked in a bookcase, with ornate and intricate details, against one wall. Its shelves were adorned with books that seemed to have a mind of their own, changing their content to suit the occupant's mood. I thought it was a nice touch, offering a bit of escapism and adventure, depending on what tickled her fancy.

Threw in loads of art supplies, scattering them about, haphazard but purposeful. Drawing and painting shite, embroidery tools, crochet and knitting materials—a right damn assortment. I figured she might have a creative streak in her and it'd be a way to keep her occupied and entertained.

And just to top it off, I stuck a fecking harp in there as well, tucked away in one corner, beckoning her with its strings. I always had a soft spot for the sweet melodies that could be coaxed from those strings. I imagined her playing a tune or two, filling the room with enchanting music.

Leaving the boudoir for the throne room, I shouted for Teàrlag. They appeared quick as a wink, likely lurking nearby. I was still cross with them, but I needed someone to tend to Moira when I couldn't, and they needed to get back in my good books.

"Tá tú i gceannas ar Moira a choinneáil sásta nuair nach bhfuil mé thart,"[75] I informed them, their feathers ruffled but keeping their bleeding trap shut. "Listen up, your job is to keep her fecking safe and sound. And none of them bollocks cock-ups like you did with the giantess. I won't

---

[75] You're in charge of keeping Moira happy when I'm not around.

tolerate any feck-ups on this one. She's my most prized possession, and I'll unleash a world of hurt if anything bleeding happens to her on your fecking watch.

You gotta make sure she's got all the grub she wants, and anything else that tickles her fancy. Keeping her happy and snug in our boudoir is your top priority until I say otherwise. I reckon you'll grow fond of her, but don't forget who's calling the damn shots here and where your fecking loyalty lies. The collar will stop her from doing any harm to herself, but it's bleeding up to you to keep her spirits high and prevent any mishaps when I'm not around. This shite shouldn't take more than a few decades. And if you do a bang-up job, I'll reward you with anything your heart desires as a token of my gratitude."

"Och aye, nae doot aboot it," Teàrlag trilled in what appeared to be genuine amusement. "I've been keepin' an ee on her, ye ken, and I reckon we'll hae a richt guid laugh. I've been pure gaspin' for some excitement in these parts, it's been donkey's years since anythin' stirred the bluid. I've got this feelin' in me banes that stickin' close tae her will hae me richt in the thick o' it!"

"Feck it all," I grumbled, my annoyance evident in my tone. "If you reckon your idea of a bleeding good time is letting her fecking prance about outside of our fecking boudoir, you better bleeding think again."

"Aye, sound, sound" they sighed, bobbed their head and shrugged. "I'll mind her as best I can, but wi' Caer

Ibormeith[76] and Lady Boann stickin' their neb in, me hauns are tied. Dinnae go takin' yer rage oot on me for somethin' I cannae control, especially onythin' tae dae wi' the Túatha Dé Danann."

"Look here, I've always been fair with the púcaí," I growled, displeased with their indifference. "You and Dunstan, you've fecking thrived under my leadership, haven't you? But don't you bleeding forget, it hasn't always been a walk in the park. Mark my words, I'll fecking tear down everything I've built if it means keeping her safe. I'm no eejit; I know you lot can't take on them damn gods and goddesses. So, keep a sharp eye on her, and the moment they come sniffing around, you fecking better come running to me, no damn questions asked."

~ Moira ~

As my eyes slowly opened, I was enveloped in a feeling of pure comfort. My eyes slowly adjusting to the dimly-lit room, I realized that I was once again in Rígán's bed. I

---

[76] Caer Ibormeith (kayr ih-bor-mayth).

couldn't resist running my hands over one of the golden tassels that hang from every corner, swaying ever so gently with each move.

I wasn't surprised he brought me back here. The light filtering through the window indicated that it was now early evening, and I wondered how long I had been asleep.

However, my attention was quickly drawn to the iron chain securely attached to the head of the bed, which was fixed to the collar around my neck. Of course, he had chained me back up, the damn bastard.

I looked down and saw he'd clothed me in a stunning lingerie set that highlighted my bountiful assets and hugged every curve. The ethereal balconette was sheer with delicate lace, intricate beading, and straps that gently wrapped around my shoulders. The matching panties were equally splendid, made of delicate lace and the waistband adorned with sparkling gemstones. To complete the set, the stunning garter belt that sat perfectly at my waist, also embellished with intricate lace and delicate beading.

Rígán had good taste in my clothing, I could give him that. He was breathtakingly handsome; anyone could see that. He even seemed clever and funny, at times. The púcaí seemed to like him well enough and even goddesses seemed to be partial to him. But none of that made him holding me captive or forcing me to want to have sex with him okay; it wasn't something I could look past to see his better qualities.

As my gaze swept across the room, I immediately noticed the additions he had made since my last 'visit'. It was as if he had meticulously orchestrated every detail, ensuring that my surroundings catered to my needs and desires while he was absent.

His lack of restraint within the room was undeniable. An impressive bookcase graced one corner, its shelves teeming with a vast collection of books that whispered tales of knowledge and wisdom. A fucking harp stood proudly, its delicate strings waiting to be awakened by skillful hands. And scattered throughout the room, an assortment of art supplies and crafting materials hinted at the potential for creative endeavors.

Curiosity getting the better of me, I slid off the bed and approached the bookshelf, the chain that bound me seeming to adapt and adjust its length accordingly within the confines of the room. It was a perplexing display of magic, responding to the environment and its inhabitants with cunning ingenuity. The more resourceful one proved to be, the more astonishing and vexing the magic became within these walls.

I perused the titles that adorned the shelves, I marveled at the sheer diversity of subjects they encompassed. Each thought that flickered through my mind was met with a book tailored to satisfy that particular yearning for knowledge. However, when it came to the books that held the potential for aiding my escape, they stubbornly remained steadfast on their shelves, refusing to budge.

Frustration coursed through my veins, my heart quickening with each failed attempt to retrieve a helpful volume. By the time the sixth book resisted my grasp, a storm of agitation consumed me. How dare Rígán confine me once again to this accursed bedroom, taunting me with

resources that were rendered useless in my quest for freedom.

Did he truly believe that a few kind gestures and the presence of a harp, of all things, would pacify my spirit?

In a fit of anger, I unleashed my fury upon the room. The easel holding a painting was toppled over, an act of defiance tinged with a sense of petty rebellion. Books, those I could successfully extract, were hurled with force, their impact shattering delicate vases and dislodging paintings from their rightful places on the walls. Bedding and velvety drapery were torn asunder, leaving the room in a state of chaotic disarray.

As I stomped around, desperately seeking another target for my destructive outburst, a searing pain jolted through my bare foot. But in an instant, the pain subsided, and I found myself transported back to the bed. The room effortlessly rearranged itself, restoring its pristine appearance as if nothing had been disturbed.

Fatigue washed over me, dampening the fires of my rage, yet frustration continued to linger. Tears streamed down my face, each sob a testament to the overwhelming sense of powerlessness that consumed me. The more I wept, the more the weight of my captivity pressed upon me, reminding me of the overwhelming odds stacked against my escape.

At that moment, time seemed distorted. Had it truly only been a day or two since my arrival? The weight of the circumstances, the limitations imposed upon me, and the realization of my own vulnerability became an unbearable burden to bear. It was an onslaught of emotions and circumstances that surpassed the threshold of my endurance, leaving me shattered and drained.

"Ya done whingin' yet, aye?" the raven looking púca, whose name I couldn't remember, tittered. I had no idea how they got in the room or how long they'd been there. "Ah thoct ye had a few mair thunderin' rants in ye afore ye gied up an' blubbered like a bairn."

"The fuck do you care?" I snapped and continued unabashedly weeping, not having the energy to collect myself or care what others thought.

"Listen, 'carin' isnae exactly the vibe I'm after here," the púca cackled, moving further into the room. "Rígán put me in charge o' ye when he's no' aboot, and frankly, it'd be pure magic if ye didnae spend the hale time moanin'. Maybe we could dae somethin' mair excitin' than hangin' aboot in yer miserable sulk."

"I honestly don't even understand most of what you just said and frankly don't really care either," I rasped, my throat sore from bawling. "Can you just fuck off, whatever your name was? I'm really not in the mood to deal with anything else."

"Aye, I'm Teàrlag," they replied. "Can't be helpin' ye if ye cannae get yer heid roon what's bein' said. Maybe try listenin' up and askin' mair questions, aye? Makin' assumptions will get ye killed roon here. Onyways, once ye're done greetin' aboot bein' treated like a bleedin' princess, which is pure pathetic, by the way, I can sort ye oot. Are ye famished? Or fancy a few pints tae numb the pain? What's wi' the feckin' harp, by the way? Want me tae teach ye how tae play the thing? Or if ye already ken, spare me the torture, will ye?"

"Ah, it is the whisper of my sixth sense that reveals unto me her predilection for my comradeship above all others," the swan lady proclaimed as she materialized in the room. "But behold, the binding link must be relinquished, for our journey calls for a greater freedom than it can bestow upon us."

The chain keeping me captive disappeared and I spared no time in rushing towards her.

Teàrlag looked absolutely petrified upon seeing her and fled with a squawk.

She might be dangerous, but she'd yet to hold me captive or force me to do anything, so I'd take my chances.

"Please take me with you," I begged, clasping her hands. "And if it's not too much to ask, maybe a change of clothes and your name?"

"Caer Ibormeith," she laughed prettily, as she transported us into an cathair ghríobháin.

I was finally in the maze and it enveloped me in its ethereal aura, the atmosphere itself seemed to acquire an enigmatic weight, as though every breath I took mingled with the very essence of magic. There was an undeniable sensation of peril that hung in the air; I couldn't help but shiver as unease crept up my spine. Each winding route carried cryptic promise, whispering tantalizing secrets that tugged at my curiosity. The very ground beneath my feet seemed to pulse with anticipation, as if it held the key to untold wonders and hidden truths, urging me onward.

Yet, it was the towering hedges that flanked me on either side that truly caught my attention. Majestic in their stature, they soared high above my head, their leaves forming an impenetrable barrier of lush greenery. The intricate patterns and entwined branches hinted at a deeper meaning; a hidden language of symbols woven into their very essence. They seemed to possess a life force of their own, a pulsating energy that resonated with the mystical forces of the world.

I noted that I now wore a white tunic, embroidered with delicate emerald vines that intertwine with shimmering golden beads. My silken skirt cascaded in soft waves around me, the colors shifting from a pastel lilac to a petal pink as I moved. My boots were supple, moss-colored, and adorned with iridescent crystals that sparkled in the sunlight. Not exactly my style, but it was better than wandering around in my underwear.

"I can't thank you enough, Caer Ibormeith," I declared, filled with gratitude. "Really, I'm in your debt."

"Ah, refer to me as Caer, my dear friend, and heed me warning as you traverse the mystical lands of Tír na nÓg," she cautioned, enveloped in an air of mystery. "I would grant you safe passage from the realm of Rígán if I could, but alas, such power is beyond my grasp, at least while you bear his collar. There are forces at work in those lands that are best left undisturbed, and I implore you to tread lightly and with great care. Those in Tír na nÓg are not to be trifled with, and one misstep could have dire consequences for you and those around you."

"I thought it was more symbolic than anything else…" I murmured, taken aback by her claim.

"Surely it's symbolic," she chortled, clearly not as distressed or surprised about the situation as I was. "It's a mesmerizing work of magic, and I've no inkling as to how he managed to get his hands on it. I don't believe he could have forged it himself... but I digress. As far as I can ascertain, the collar shackles you to his side, restricting your movements beyond the limits of his realm unless he permits it.

The iron it's forged from suppresses your magic, but it seems your longevity, youth, and natural resilience as a Bean Sí remains intact. However, you'll scarcely discover your full potential for centuries to come, even if the collar were removed, as you learn to wield untamed magic and sharpen your will and intent. The piece is also imbued with wards for safety and good fortune, and I'm certain there are more secrets lurking within. Truly, it's an exquisite masterpiece of artistry."

Fuckity, fuck, fuck, fuck. I was so fucked. In just every way possible.

"Ah, sure now, wouldn't it be a grand idea to take a saunter through an cathair ghríobháin, and have a bit of a chat?" she cajoled, knowing I could only say yes. "You could consider it as payment for my previous assistance in rescuing you, my dear friend. I must say, I do find myself quite fond of your company. It's as if your presence aids in the clarity of my thoughts, allowing me to see my path forward with greater ease. And fear not, for there is no danger to be found here, so long as we are together. And with that collar adorning your neck and the protection of Rígán, even if we were to be separated, you would likely remain unharmed."

Chapter Twelve

~ Rígán ~

I sussed out the moment Caer Ibormeith rocked up in my castle. I was already trying to keep myself in check, not showing any reaction to Moira's pure rage and then despair, even though it was tearing my soul apart. I knew she needed some time to get used to her situation, and I was hoping Teàrlag could help with that in ways I hadn't managed yet. But then Caer Ibormeith swooped in and snatched her away.

If an Dagda hadn't shown up at the same time, I might have made it in time to put a stop to the whole thing. They were in an cathair ghríobháin, which didn't worry me as much as all them damn Túatha Dé Danann running amok on my land. The fact that an Dagda was in my midst was downright fecking terrifying. If I could've bolted to Moira, I would've.

189

An Dagda, was a proper legend, revered as a father-figure and the first king of the Túatha Dé Danann. He went by many names, like the Great God, Horseman, Great Father, Mighty One, and Lord of Great Knowledge. An Dagda was the epitome of all things grand and powerful. He was known for being the embodiment of fertility, husbandry, manliness, strength, magic, druidry, and wisdom.

No matter that he hadn't done much or blabbed much yet, except for keeping me trapped in my throne room, I could feel his raw power and I knew I was outmatched. No doubt about it. If I wanted to walk out of this meeting in one piece, I'd better tread lightly and keep him pleased. No room for mucking about.

Still, every bone in my body was screaming at me to sod the consequences and go after Moira. Make sure she was safe and do whatever it took to keep her that way. Keeping her hidden away just wasn't doing the damn trick.

An Dagda, now there was a proper sight to behold! He was a bleeding giant, with the strength to match. He had a face as rough as a badger's arse, I swear! And the fella was as pale as the moon itself, with them brown eyes that could see right through you. His mop of gray hair cascaded in waves down his massive shoulders, and that beard of his, holy feck, it was longer than a winter's night!

The cloak he had on was a real work of art. Made from fancy fabric with all these intricate designs that would make your eyes pop out. It draped over him, flowing all the way down to the ground. Underneath that cloak, he was sporting a robe that was just as fancy, covered in symbols and patterns that screamed of power.

Stories about an Dagda were always spreading like wildfire, talking about his amazing powers. The fella had control over life and death, the weather and crops, and could even mess with time and the seasons. His club was a proper deadly weapon, reckon it could take down nine blokes with one swing or bring them back from the dead. And his cauldron, it was bottomless, could fill up any man's belly. His harp, a work of art, made from the finest oak and could command whole armies. He had not one, but two magical pigs. One just kept growing and growing, like there was no end to it, and the other was always sizzling on the spit, ready for a feast. His fruit trees, they never ran outta fruit. But what everyone wanted the most was that black-maned heifer he had. When she mooed for her calf, all the cattle in Ireland would come grazing, bringing abundance to the whole land.

With all of these deadly gifts and abilities, an Dagda was a proper legend of immense power and wisdom, respected and revered by all the feckers who knew of him.

"Ah, Rígán, I trust you are fully aware of the purpose that brings me to your presence. I would greatly prefer to avoid any further struggles in order to secure your company within this chamber," an Dagda declared with an air that tolerated no scrutiny. "Nevertheless, in the event that my words have not yet penetrated your understanding, I stand ready to employ more drastic measures, including the chaining of your person to the floor and the adoption of a more forceful demeanor. You see, Boann has implored me to ensure that mo mac óg receives your invaluable assistance. It has been deeply impressed upon me that the bond between your Moira and Caer Ibormeith holds paramount importance in this undertaking."

I snarled my comprehension, but I reckon I didn't quite hit the mark of showing respect. It'd been donkey's years since I last lost control, but recent days had me acting like a complete eejit once more. Moira's arrival, and then that bloody damn ceremony, had knocked me off my feet.

"Ah, I do vividly recall the moment my eyes first beheld the bewitching beauty of Boann," an Dagda let out a rather nostalgic grunt "Therefore, I shall grant you some latitude in your emotional display towards me on this occasion. However, let it be known that my memory is as sharp as my wit, and I shall retain in my recollection every uttered word and every enacted deed of this day."

~ Moira ~

Caer and I walked through the dusk of an cathair ghríobháin in affable silence for a while, comfortable and in no rush to get to any particular destination. As we wandered the twists and turns of the maze, we found ourselves standing at the entrance of a breathtakingly beautiful ancient garden.

The air was filled with the sweet fragrance of blooming flowers, and the soft rustling of leaves and chirping of birds provided a peaceful symphony that soothed the soul. The garden itself was a wonder to behold, with tall, graceful trees reaching for the sky, numerous torches lighting the area, and winding paths leading to hidden nooks and crannies filled with stunning blooms. The colors were rich and vibrant, with a rainbow of hues painting the landscape. Roses, lilies, and irises were just a few of the many species that filled the garden, each one carefully cultivated and seemingly tended to with love and care.

Nestled amidst the foliage of the garden, there was a quaint sitting area that beckoned me to take a seat and relax.

The space was cozy yet open, with a small lantern-lit metal table surrounded by comfortable looking chairs that had plush cushions in shades of deep green and soft cream. It struck me as a place that made you want to stay forever, lost in the beauty and serenity around you.

"Ah, what a beguiling garden to be discovered amidst this mundane labyrinth, my dear friend," Caer remarked as she took a seat at the table. "It is a ponderous thought indeed, why Rígán felt the need to conjure such an intricate maze. Undoubtedly, it is a mesmerizing and potent manifestation of sorcery. Yet one cannot help but question its true purpose and significance for the enigmatic Rígán."

I had no answer for her. I didn't know Rígán well enough to speculate and "An Cathair Ghríobháin" had never mentioned it. Admittedly, I had also never really spared a thought for his reasoning.

"Ah sure, one might wonder, why on earth would anyone go to the trouble of erecting obstructions to keep others out?" she pondered, looking at me as if I could shed any light on the topic. "The púcaí, you see, don't appear to have any issues with wandering in and out of this place, although most of them tend to confine themselves within the city's limits. Of course, my dear friend, it's not as if there's any way for him to bar the Túatha Dé Danann from entering or exiting, so that can't be the motive behind it. It could be that it presents a challenge to other Aes Sídhe or lesser beings. Perhaps it's simply for the sake of amusement, with no other purpose beyond that."

"I'm sure I don't know," I remarked, not particularly interested in the subject. "This is actually my first time within it."

"Well now, isn't that a curious thing to hear, my dear friend," she quipped, as if there were a deeper meaning to her words. "I've found myself frequenting these parts as of late. However, and I daresay you won't be taken aback by this, I hold a greater fondness for the lake where our paths first crossed."

"I see," I acknowledged, unsure where this was all going.

"Ah, my dear friend, it seems our discussion must be postponed until another occasion," she announced abruptly and vanished.

I was distinctly less relaxed without her presence. The garden was still serene, but it no longer mirrored my emotional state. Jarringly, all of my previous anxieties, turmoil, and fears were reasserting themselves.

As I worried over why Caer left so abruptly and my next steps, an imposing figure with flaming red hair, hazel eyes, and commanding presence joined me in the garden. He made no pretense of not noticing me as he stomped towards where I was sitting.

He wore a fine robe of vibrant purple that was adorned with intricate embroidery and gemstones. His woolen cloak was trimmed with fur and decorated with intricate patterns.

Twisted golden bands encircled his neck and biceps, and he was bedecked with rings and bracelets that were set with precious gems.

"Bodb Derg[77]," he greeted me, with a thick Irish accent, his fiery gaze just as likely to strike fear into the hearts of his enemies as to inspire devotion. "Allow me to introduce myself. That is my name. As I surmise you are not acquainted with me, I generally do not find it necessary to present myself."

"Ope, hello," I sputtered, very wary of him. "I'm Moira Boyne."

"Indeed, I am aware," Bodb stated and took a seat across from me. "As the King of the Túatha Dé Danann and commander of both the heavens and the earth below, very little escapes my notice. Especially not comely maidens newly arrived in Tír na nÓg."

"It's nice to meet you, your majesty," I lied and hoped for the best. "I should actually be on my way though…"

"Don't be running off just yet, my dear." His voice was deep and resonant, imbued with a natural authority that left no room for disobedience or dissent. "Let us dispense with the formalities, I insist you address me as Bo. I would like to become better acquainted with you. It appears you have a significant role to play in these parts."

"Ope, I wouldn't say that," I hedged.

---

[77] Bodb Derg (bove jehrg).

"How terribly modest of you, my dear," he said with a grin. "It's quite becoming in a lady. To my dismay, I've heard that you are bound to Rígán."

I wasn't sure how to answer him. He seemed dangerous and I wasn't sure how to act around him. It made me realize that as much as I despised Rígán, I always felt safe, although I shouldn't, around him. I never felt the need to pretend or act a certain way in his presence and as much as he took away my autonomy and didn't care about my consent, I didn't think he actually wanted to maliciously hurt me.

Even in short absences, I found myself yearning for his presence against my better judgment. I didn't understand how I could find him so contemptuous and yet only feel whole when I was near him.

He was certainly possessive; but in his own peculiar manner, it was evident that he was making sincere efforts to look after me. There was no denying that he managed to make me feel not just desired but profoundly attractive, though it came with its own toxicity.

Ultimately, I struggled to accept any relationship that demanded I gave up my autonomy or overlooked abuse. Yet, I was also all too aware that my own desires on that front might not matter in the face of literal magic.

"Deineann ceann ciallmhar béal iadhta,"[78] he interrupted my thoughts to tell me. "However, I'm afraid a lack of response simply won't suffice. Pray tell, what measures may I take to assist in unlocking your tongue, my dear?"

---

[78] A wise head makes a closed mouth.

"It's just a complicated topic." I shrugged, wanting to appease him and leave as quickly as possible. "Technically, we are soul bonded, I suppose? That's what I've been told at least."

"You do not have affection for him?" he probed, leaning uncomfortably close to me.

"I wouldn't say that," I stammered, not wanting him to think I was available to his advances. "We're just having some growing pains, like any new relationship…"

"I have heard it's more than mere growing pains, my dear," he commented.

"From whom?" I couldn't help but ask.

"That's not important, my dear," he huffed, waving off my question. "I hear a great many things. What truly matters is whether they are true. I have heard that love is blind to blemishes and faults. Ceileann searc ainimh is locht.[79] Is that not the case for you and Rígán?"

"I'm not sure it's wise to idealize anyone, particularly not someone you are planning on spending the rest of your life in a partnership with," I replied honestly. "But I can see how desire might temporarily override better judgment or deceive us into believing negative traits are not deal breakers."

"My goodness, how cynical of you," he laughed heartily. "Do you not believe in soulmates? I daresay it's not a particularly Irish concept, but the two of you prove that there are a few out there."

---

[79] Love is blind to blemishes and faults.

"I suppose," I answered noncommittally.

"Mas duine glic tú gabh comairie,"[80] he demanded and I wasn't about to ask for a translation. "Embrace the fires of contention, dissonance, and subsequent reconciliation."

"I'm not sure I understand," I said hesitantly.

"My dear, if you wish to thrive in Tír na nÓg, you must unlock the doors of your heart to your partner and forge a bond of steel," he said as if that cleared everything up. "Align your needs with your partner's primal urges through negotiation. Inquire diligently, lest presumptions poison your relations. Contemplate before speaking, lest hasty words bring ruin."

Did he want Rígán and I to work out or not? Did I even really have a choice in the long run? If I could get past what Rígán had done to me, did I want us to work out? Were his violations something I was willing to get past?

"I appreciate the advice," I assured him and started to get up from my seat. "I'll do my best to use it wisely."

"Are you departing so soon?" he asked and rose as well. "I would relish the opportunity to become better acquainted with you."

"That is more kindness than I deserve," I insisted and tried to back towards the garden's entrance. "I should probably go put your advice to good use while it's so fresh in my mind."

---

[80] If you are wise, take advice.

"My dear, that is a most delightful thought," he remarked and easily closed the distance between us. "However, it would hardly be gentlemanly of me to allow you to make your own way back to Rígán. Allow me the honor of escorting you there myself."

He took me by the arm and I found myself back in Rígán's throne room. My relief that he followed through on his word was quickly lost as the sight that awaited me was far from what I'd expected.

An overwhelming sense of dread washed over me. There, in the center of the room, stood a colossal figure who exuded an overpowering amount of dominance. It was as if the very air had grown heavy, charged with an unworldly force.

This giant of a man loomed over Rígán, who knelt on the floor, battered and bruised. Chains clinked as they restrained Rígán's wrists, securing him to the cold stone beneath him. The metal cuffs dug into his flesh, leaving deep impressions and chafed skin.

The sight of him made my heart ache; he looked so broken and defenseless.

Rígán's eyes roved over me, taking in everything and causing my core to heat. I hated that I still desired him so much, even in his current battered state, and entirely without his intervention.

This was clearly no ordinary encounter; it was a clash of titanic forces, and Rígán was not the victor. The contrast between the two figures was stark; Rígán, once proud and formidable, now reduced to a bloodied captive, while this untamed beast of a man stood as a force of nature over him.

Bruises bloomed across Rígán's face, a canvas of purples, blues, and blacks that spoke of the physical blows he'd endured. Blood trickled down from his split lip, evidence of a more recent struggle. I noticed the swollen and puffy state of his eyes, suggesting that he had taken severe punches. His cheekbones appeared reddened and tender, likely the result of a powerful strike that had landed squarely on the zygomatic bone.

Seeing Rígán at the mercy of this formidable man filled me with a mix of helplessness and desperation.

Torn fabric revealed patches of exposed skin, where his body had suffered additional cuts and abrasions. The depth of his wounds hinted at the intensity of the struggle, the physical pain he had endured.

I longed to rush to his side, to free him from his restraints and shield him from any further harm. I loathed how deeply concerned I was for him.

But the sheer magnitude of this man's presence, his overwhelming strength, left me paralyzed.

"Father, it seems that things are going swimmingly," Bobd observed with a smirk. "Have you finished conversing with Rígán? I have returned with his delightful lady."

"Ah, my dear compatriots, Rígán and I have partaken in a most enlightening discourse, mayhaps," the man's rich Irish accent boomed and echoed through the room. "I dare say, we have reached a harmonious understanding on a multitude of affairs."

"I reckon you're keeping yourself in good spirits, mo shíorghra?" Rígán drawled as if nothing was amiss.

Rígán's posture, though submissive in the face of that man's overwhelming presence, still retained a glimmer of defiance. Despite his injuries, I could see the stubborn determination in his eyes, a refusal to yield completely.

"I'd be more concerned with myself, if I were you," I couldn't help but snip back at him as he was clearly fine enough to bicker.

"Fear not, mo bhuanghrá, an Dagda has been mighty generous with his wisdom," he grunted and spit blood to the floor. "But what truly lifts my spirits is having you back in my circle. Your absence was like a kick in the bollocks, I tell you."

"Lo and behold, my progeny!" an Dagda crowed in delight. "We have attained a state of flawless concord! Let us gracefully withdraw, allowing these lovebirds their well-deserved solitude."

Chapter Thirteen

~ Rígán ~

After an Dagda buggered off, I finally managed to free myself from the damn chains and slumped into a more comfortable seated position.

Moira cautiously made her way over, her face showing genuine concern. It was a relief to see her giving a shite about my well-being.

"Can you heal yourself?" she asked, all earnest and caring.

"Wait a tick," I wheezed through the agony of my injuries, no longer bothering to feign ignorance of an Dagda's brutalities. "My whole body's sore, and I'm wrecked from enduring the fecking attentions of our Great God, mo shíorghra, just to reach you."

"I wasn't able to sense your distress…" she mumbled and took a seat beside me. "Were you cut off from me too? You should have been able to feel that I was safe. Caer and Bo were with me the whole time. Though I didn't care much for Bo's company and Caer did just leave me to him."

"Caer and Bo, eh?" I grunted, feeling a twinge of jealousy, even though I knew she was destined to love only me. "Mo bhuanghrá, forgive me for grunting, but can I ask if you're giving pet names to every Tom, Dick, and Harry now? I'm bleeding sure an Dagda had something to do with me not being able to sense your emotional state or your presence in our fecking realm through our bond."

"Our realm?" she repeated, sounding gobsmacked.

"Aye, mo shíorghra, you're my other half, and I call the shots around here," I huffed, wondering why it wasn't as clear to her as it was to me. "That makes you the Queen of the púcaí, even if you aren't one of them."

"I don't feel like I rule anything here, not even my own self," she contended, giving me a withering look.

"Oh?" I grumbled, knowing full well this was gonna be blamed on me.

"Wouldn't you feel that way if you were continually assaulted, locked up in a room, and treated like someone's plaything?" she seethed, her rage radiating off her.

"Ah now, don't be such a diva," I scoffed, thinking she was acting like she'd been scarred for life.

All I've done was treat her like royalty and put her on a pedestal in my world.

205

"Fuck you, I'm not being a diva!" she roared and mo bod twitched, captivated by her stunning beauty even in the middle of a row. "Godsdammit, stop that! I'm not in the mood, just like every other damn time!"

"I always ensure your craic is top-notch and your wants are catered for, mo bhuanghrá," I reminded her, trying to make her see.

"Look, it's apparent to me that you're not getting this," she fumed and mo bod was positively a-quiver with each of her withering stares. "I'm not disputing that my body liked what happened. I have very little control over that, as you made quite sure whether you meant to or not. What I am saying is that I, am a person not just your sex toy, do not like being forced into a trance in which I lose control over myself in every way. You say you love me, but I can't see how that is possible since you just met me, know nothing about who I really am, never ask me what I want, and don't seem to care when you're hurting me! That is not love."

"Listen up, mo bhuanghrá, it was you who made the promise and got yourself into this mess," I grumbled, getting fed up with the same old blather. "I'm not the one holding the magic, nor do I have any control over it. But if you willingly surrender yourself to me, the magic won't mess with your enjoyment. It only brings out what's needed to make you feel pleasure and desire."

"Great, I'm sure that is all true," she hissed, clearly displeased. "But if you want me to love you or ever be here willingly, you're going to have to earn it, not just try to force it from me. I promise you, time will not make me change my mind on this. I will always demand my autonomy."

"Well, mo shíorghra, you may argue that's the case, but I'm afraid I have a firmer grip on the whims of time than you do," I teased, not relishing her despondency, yet unwilling to concede on a matter she clearly lacked the perspective to comprehend. "I've lived through countless ages, experiencing the full gamut of helplessness, enslavement, thrashings, adoration, might, and dominion over others."

"You would think that would give you a better perspective then!" she objected, shifting herself further away from my presence.

I was wrecked, completely knackered, and there was no way in bleeding hell I could handle fighting on two fronts. My head was spinning, trying to figure out how to keep Moira safe while dealing with them Túatha Dé Danann gobshites.

Maybe, if she was up for it, she could even lend me a hand dealing with those persistent buggers who just wouldn't bugger off, always sticking their noses in our business no matter what I did. I needed her on the same page as me, so we could face this shite together and keep each other outta harm's way.

"Ah, go on then, spill the beans, what is it you fancy?" I asked, genuinely intrigued and finding a good laugh in the puzzled look on her gob.

"I don't know everything I want," she sighed, sounding a bit down. "I'm not used to not having life goals. But I know that I want to be treated like a full person who makes decisions in their own life. I want whoever I'm with to care about my opinion, needs, and desires. I don't want to ever be in that trance-like state again, unless I ask to be. And if we're together, in any capacity, I want it to be because we chose it and worked for it - not because I was bound and forced to."

"Right then, I suppose we'll give it a go," I conceded, curious to see how things would pan out, and well aware that in the end, I had the upper hand. "I can't undo the magic or the spell that's been cast, but I'll do my best to make sure you don't slip into a trance-like state without your say-so, mo bhuanghrá. I might not fully grasp why all this means so much to you, but that's neither here nor there. What matters is that you're happy, and I'm game to give this a shot. I won't even entertain the thought of us being apart, but I'll do my best to court you if that's what you're after."

"I'm not really sure how to respond to all of that," she admitted with a touch of sadness. "There is a part of me that wants to thank you and start over and a part of me that still thinks that is all just the bare minimum and how could I ever forgive you for what you've done."

"Well, mo shíorghra, my vote is for the former," I bantered, and she kindly let me come closer to her.

"Can I try something?" she pleaded, her gaze firm and determined. "I want to know how much of everything I felt was really me and how much was my body making me enjoy us being together. I think I need to know to figure out how to move forward. But I have to be the one in control, no magic or doing anything without anything without me telling you to."

"I'd never refuse you, mo shíorghra, and I'll make sure you don't slip into a daze," I promised eagerly, more than happy to indulge in whatever she willingly offered at that moment.

Moira approached me, tearing off a piece of fabric from the bleeding awful clothes some eejit had given her. She dabbed at the blood on my face, gentle as a lamb with the meager materials she had on hand. Truth be told, I could've tended to myself just fine, but I savored every moment of her tending to me nonetheless.

Once she finished tending to my bloody mess, she lobbed the rag aside and hopped right onto my lap. She gently stroked my face and mane, meticulously exploring my horns and ears.

Her eyes glanced up to meet mine, and I could feel her desire surge through our connection, but I had to keep my own urges in check, not wanting to overpower her.

Ever so gently, she pressed her lips against mine, and the sensation of her mouth on mine electrified my entire being.

Her moans and hands gripping my shirt intensified my desire for her, but didn't seem to overpower her own.

Wrapping her arms around my neck, she intensified our kiss, giving me the green light to ravish her.

She threw me for six by breaking our kiss and making a beeline for my neck, peppering kisses along my jawline and tracing her tongue along my pulse.

I played it cool, keeping my hands on her waist, waiting for her to take the lead.

With the precision of a surgeon, she deftly undid the buttons on my waistcoat and I helped her slide it off my back.

There was no hiding the fact that mo bod was dying for her touch, yearning for her in every way possible.

She wasted no time in getting her hands under my shirt, tracing the contours of my abs and chest. Every touch sent shivers down my spine and left me gasping for more.

When she gave me the nod, I peeled my shirt off, leaving my torso exposed for her to explore.

I was positively gasping to divest her of her vestments, but I resisted my inclinations to demonstrate my dependability and grant her authority. It was a grand sensation, far surpassing my wildest imaginations, to have her present whilst we were intertwined. Everything I once deemed flawless was now elevated with her attentions not solely fixated on indulging my own desires.

Mo bod was in a right state, harder than I've ever known.

As she took me in, my entire being pulsated in unison with her ardor. Fortunately, my needs didn't overpower hers and she kept complete mastery. The more she fixed her gaze, the more apprehensive I grew lest she prolong it beyond my restraint.

At last, she cradled my visage and assailed me with her lips, and we both sniggered as our teeth clashed in agony. Her cheeks went crimson, and I was quite taken with the sight.

~ Moira ~

I felt like a bumbling teenager making out with her first crush. I needed to be in control, at least this time, but was overwhelmed with the prospect. My body, arousal, needs, all my own, were all in overdrive.

His presence was like an addiction, overriding any reasoning or prudence I would generally have in similar situations. I hated how easy it would be for me to forgive him anything. I wasn't weak willed or tolerant of abuse, but when it came to him it was so very difficult to hold on to anything but positive sentiments.

I ground myself against his cock, hands on his shoulders, writhing in his lap until I was ready to combust.

Our moans mingled and interspersed with panting need.

Rígán rutted into me a little harder than before, hitting me just right, and I came undone, nails digging into his shoulders and chest arching into his.

"That was kinda embarrassing," I gasped into the crook of his neck.

"Jaysus, mo bhuanghrá, that was fecking grand," he sighed into my hair, wrapping me in his strong arms. "How're you holding up? Might we persevere a bit longer?"

"Can we maybe eat instead?" I asked, both hungry and wanting to see if he would put his needs to the side when asked. "I'm a bit famished…"

"Aye, it's been a fecking long day, and the hour is getting late," he acknowledged under strain. "So, tell me, do ye have any demands or something?"

I pulled back from him to search his face. I needed to know how much of this was because he was genuinely turning over a new leaf or was just trying to placate me in the short-term.

He seemed unhappy but genuine, but there was no way for me to tell why he acquiesced.

"Um, I'm pretty open to anything…" I mumbled as I wondered whether the bond would tell me if he was lying to me. "Can you do me a quick favor and tell me a lie, but like you are trying hard to deceive me."

"What?" he questioned, clearly confused by my random request. "I'd never pull the wool over your eyes. What's the bleeding point? You'd suss it out quick as a wink, just like I'd do if you were to keep something from me on purpose."

That was something to continue to think about. It certainly would be a useful thing to understand about our connection. If he was lying about lying, our bond certainly wasn't alerting me to anything.

"Mo shíorghra, would you kindly get up?" he morosely requested. "Though I'd rather you stay put so we can carry on with our earlier business, if that isn't an option, I'll need a moment to sort my head out for the next feed."

I scooted off his lap, he rose, and I felt a little guilty when I saw him painfully adjust himself in his pants.

He offered me his hand to help me up. I accepted, happy for the assistance.

It was always fascinating to watch Rígán conjure up something from nothing. The air was thick with the scent of roses and other sweet flowers, their petals strewn across the floor in a carpet of crimson and gold. We were surrounded by a chorus of ethereal voices, singing songs of love and devotion.

A huge, intricately carved baroque table appeared, surrounded by matching chairs with plush red velvet cushions. The table was laden with exotic delicacies, the likes of which I had never seen before. Succulent fruits, rare meats, and fragrant herbs were arranged in artful patterns, while delicate crystal goblets sparkled in the flickering candlelight.

Rígán smiled as my eyes widened in delight.

He gestured for me to sit, and as I did, he lifted a bottle of shimmering liquid and poured it into my goblet. Taking a sip, I moaned with appreciation, it was the most delicious wine I'd ever tasted, as a warm feeling spread throughout my body.

He sat down opposite me, and we began to eat; the food was exquisite, each dish a work of art.

~ Rígán ~

Whilst Moira slumbered on, I made my way to tend to our guest. I could feel his arrival, and I was proper eager to be done with him. Leaving our love nest and making my way to the throne room was no easy task. I'd much rather just bask in the sight of her peaceful slumber.

Aye, if it were up to me, last night would've taken a different turn. A cozy dinner and snuggling up together was grand. I enjoyed every bit of it, but it wasn't exactly how I would've planned the evening. Mind you, seeing Moira smile so freely and laugh so heartily after her previous gloomy state was a sight to behold, I'll give you that. Now, I'm left yearning for her genuine desire.

When I got to Aengus Óg[81], there he was, sprawled on my throne, looking all too cozy.

The lad, as per usual, was a good fist shorter than myself, looked to be in his twenties, with a sun-kissed complexion, curly golden locks, and eyes as blue as the ocean. It's true that many deem him a handsome fecker, but I always found him a bit of a bother to look at.

And today, to make it worse, the cheeky fecker had the audacity to wear a crown of flowers on his noggin, a fancy

---

[81] Aengus Óg (eng-us ohg).

breastplate with shiny gems over his tunic, trousers, and a cloak all decked out with flowers and leaves and such fancy shite.

He was a right charming devil, known for his silver tongue and knack for making people swoon and pledge their hearts to him. They say he's a master of poetry and music, with a voice like sweet honey that could enchant even the most jaded of hearts.

Being the youngest son of an Dagda, he always struck me as a spoilt little gobshite who never had to face the real world.

"Ah, Rígán, it's an honor you grace me with your presence at last!" he beamed in his friendly way. "I feared I would wait indefinitely here, yearning for the pleasure of your arrival."

"It's only been a bleeding minute since you got here," I grumbled, rolling my eyes.

"My dearest companion, you know well the worth of your company," he insisted, rising from my throne with open arms for a hug. "Are you not the most enchanting of friends, whose presence brings joy till daylight's fade?"

I gave him a half-hearted embrace. We were mates, but it wasn't like we were on the same level, and I didn't exactly enjoy our little gatherings. He treated me decent, seemed to genuinely appreciate our friendship and all, but I couldn't stand being around folks who could just snap their fingers and make me disappear like a ghost.

"Why are you here at this ungodly hour?" I griped, pulling away from his grasp.

"Do not pretend ignorance with me," he crowed. "You know full well why I'm here. My father, mother, and brother have confided in you. Forgive me, my dearest companion, but they tend to falter when I'm perturbed."

How the feck anyone could tell he was bothered was beyond me. Maybe his family had this uncanny ability to sniff out a different side of him or read his moods better than I ever could. Whenever we were together, I mainly focused on surviving his presence and enjoying any perks that came with his existence.

"It's plain as day you're all after Caer Ibormeith," I remarked. "I'm amazed she's managed to elude and evade you for so long."

"Indeed, I beseeched their approval to take the lead," he sighed, but then perked up. "Granted, I sought my cherished ancestors' guidance to find mo sméar iúr[82] once more. But I'm optimistic about reclaiming her. I rely on your favor now that she resides within your realm."

---

[82] Mo sméar iúr (moh smayr yoor): My yew berry.

Chapter Fourteen

~ Moira ~

I was still on edge when I woke up, not willing to let my guard down.

Rígán had been true to his word last night, going so far as to not touch me without my permission. Still, that wasn't even an entire day of changed behavior and again, kinda below the bare minimum I was looking for in the beginning of a serious relationship.

Stretching, I checked to make sure I wasn't chained to the bed again - thankfully I was not.

Sitting up, I realized I had on nothing but the nightgown Rígán had provided upon my request before bed. It was of his design, but he'd at least asked what I was looking for in regards to its creation.

The nightgown was a soft gray color, had an ethereal look to it, and felt luxuriously silky against my skin. As was his taste, he'd embellished it with intricate embroidery and the bodice was adorned with shimmering beads. The floor-length skirt that billowed around me as I moved from the bed towards the door.

I wasn't sure what I should do with my time or where I wanted to be, but I was drawn to finding Rígán. When I wasn't using all of my energy to fight against or despise him, my being felt the need to be near him. I could only surmise this was again some effect of the bonding magic as I'd never felt this way about anyone else before.

Yet again, I was forced to contemplate whether it mattered why I felt or wanted or accepted certain things, or just that I did. Certainly, it was infuriating to have the autonomy of my own desires and feelings taken from me, but at the end of the day they all felt like they were originating from me.

I could no longer be sure of the authenticity of anything I experienced, but I still had to live through it as the only form of reality I knew.

I could absolutely analyze and work diligently to oppose experiences that didn't align with my sense of self, it's what I had been doing since Boann bound me to Rígán. However, it was becoming more and more difficult to determine what was real and what was artifice.

Would my time and energy be better spent learning how to accept what I felt, regardless of its origins, or would that lead me to completely losing who I was?

Boann had assured us that we would retain our individuality, which could mean what I felt was truly coming from me, it just may be exacerbated by magic to make our joining occur in a more expedited manner. She had also said Rígán wouldn't be able to harm me and I heartily disagreed with her understanding on that subject.

I desperately wished there was a clear-cut answer to all of this.

As I walked through the castle's hallways, somewhat aimlessly, I more carefully observed my surroundings then when I'd toured them last. The walls and ceiling were adorned with ornate frescoes and intricate stucco work, depicting scenes from what I would have considered Irish mythology. The inner hallways were illuminated by crystal and candle chandeliers hanging from the ceiling or golden sconces upon the walls, that cast a warm glow on the polished marble floors.

My location became a bit more familiar and I could hear voices coming from ahead of me. I walked into the throne room and found Rígán talking with some ridiculously handsome man. It was clear they were both aware of my presence before I was of theirs.

"Ah, the enigmatic Moira, of whom I've been told tales," the gorgeous blond man chuckled and I blushed as he looked me over. "Does she always welcome her guests in such celestial attire?"

"Mo bhuanghrá," Rígán began, "would you fancy a more suitable getup for greeting our 'esteemed guest,' Aengus Óg of the Túatha Dé Danann?"

"Sure," I sputtered, not sure how to react around Aengus Óg. "Maybe something with pants?"

My nightgown transformed into an exceedingly comfortable and flattering outfit. The purple blouse was silken with delicate details along the scooped neckline, which showed more cleavage than I was used to, and tucked into high-waisted pants. The pants were olive drab linen, tailored to fit my form, with a slight flare at the hem to allow for ease of movement. The outfit was completed with a pair of wooden-colored sandals adorned with crystals.

How he could spend so much energy dressing me and still end up wearing the same variation of his own outfit every day, I couldn't understand. I felt like I'd seen at least three different versions of his black cloak, long-sleeved open linen shirt, black waistcoat, gray pants, and boots. It seemed oddly boring of him to not mix it up more often.

"Thank you," I offered with a smile, hoping praise would keep him on the straight and narrow.

"Of course, mo shíorghra," he snorted in delight, "I'll give you a bit of info about our guest here so you know him a tad better, cause he'd be right pissed if I didn't. Aengus Óg is the bleeding god of youth, love, summertime, and poetry. Some call him the Young Son, cause he's the youngest spawn of an Dagda. You might've already figured out that Boann is his mammy. He's on a fecking quest to find Caer Ibormeith."

"Ope, damn," I sighed, starting to put the pieces together.

"Surely, you'll assist me in seeking mo sméar iúr," Aengus Óg asserted with mirth. "I've heard she holds a fondness for you, Moira. I'm intrigued to discover the thoughts you share, and why she favors your company over mine, causing a hint of envy to stir within."

"Ah," I hesitantly began, Aengus Óg seemed to be in a good mood but I wasn't sure he would remain in one if I refused him. "I'm not really comfortable helping you with that…"

"Mo bhuanghrá, we're fecking obligated to help him out with this mess," Rígán cautioned me with a pained expression. "I am certain that Caer Ibormeith comprehends the situation; she can't bleeding hide forever."

"Ah, my dearest companion, your penchant for theatrics is truly divine," Aengus Óg quipped with a playful eye roll. "Mo sméar iúr and I have merely stumbled upon a misunderstanding, yet the world has turned it into a grand spectacle. But fear not, once I converse with her, all shall be set right. My dearest companion, I beseech you, where might I find her now?"

"Fecking an cathair ghríobháin," Rígán huffed in annoyance. "I can take us to the place she's at, but I can't guarantee a smooth reunion; that's between you two. I need your damn word that no matter how this shite pans out, you won't blame Moira or me for the outcome."

"Indeed, I assure you!" pledged Aengus Óg. "What folly you display on this day."

~ Rígán ~

The verdant field was a picturesque and peaceful spot, a right beauty compared to an cathair ghríobháin's corridors. I had created it to break up the endless monotony of hedges and walls. If it managed to lull someone into abandoning their quest, well, that was even better.

The grass was a lush green, swaying gently in the breeze, adorned with wildflowers of every color. The butterflies were having a grand old time, flitting about like carefree souls. And scattered around the place were a few trees, providing a bit of shade and shelter, their leaves rustling softly in the wind. The gentle hum of bees and the cheerful chirping of birds filled the air, creating a tranquil atmosphere that could soothe the weariest of souls.

Right in the middle of the field, I had placed a wee pond, many moons ago. It always shimmered, whether in the golden sun or the silvery moonlight. The water was crystal clear, showing off the smooth stones lining the pond's bottom and the playful fish darting to and fro. It was the very definition of idyllic, a place where peace and serenity reigned supreme.

"Ah, alas! The countenance of mo sméar iúr eludes my gaze," Aengus Óg bemoaned upon arrival. "Pray, my dearest companion, are you certain of her presence?"

"She was here," I retorted in exasperation. "She's a fecking fast one, evidently not yet prepared to receive either of us."

"Where has my mo sméar iúr vanished?" Aengus Óg inquired with a hint of concern, though his smile remained intact. "Let us hasten to find her and entrap her!"

"Cease your incessant whinging, my 'dearest friend'," I grumbled, unwilling to involve myself in this malarkey, as I had more pressing matters to attend to. "She's in the damn spooked timberland now."

"Oh, my dearest companion, how I relish the way you bestow upon me such a gracious mention," Aengus Óg endeavored to compliment me. "Might we hasten forthwith?"

~ Moira ~

When we arrived in the forest, the first thing that greeted me was the thick and eerie mist that hung in the air. It gave the whole area a mysterious and foreboding atmosphere, as if unseen terrors lurked within its depths.

The gnarled and twisted trees stood like ancient sentinels, their branches reaching out in twisted formations, casting long, eerie shadows on the forest floor. The dim light that managed to penetrate the dense canopy created a patchwork of illumination, showing off patches of moss and fallen leaves, while the rest of the forest remained shrouded in darkness.

As we walked through the forest, I couldn't shake the feeling that I was not alone. The rustling of leaves and the snapping of branches echoed through the stillness, sending shivers down my spine. I would turn around, expecting to see someone or something, but there was nothing there. Yet, the sense of being watched persisted, as if unseen eyes followed my every move.

Moment by moment the darkness seemed to intensify, and the twistedness of the surroundings became more pronounced. The shadows danced and flickered along the forest floor, taking on shapes that seemed to shift and morph, playing tricks on my mind. The path twisted and turned unpredictably, leading us into what felt like uncharted territory.

It became increasingly difficult to discern reality from illusion, as the line between the natural and the supernatural blurred within the depths of the haunted forest. The forest seemed alive, teeming with unseen malevolence. It was as if the very essence of the place echoed with the whispers of forgotten tales and the restless spirits of the past.

The scent that filled the air added to the eerie ambiance of the forest. The earthy aroma of damp soil and decaying leaves mingled with the lingering scent of ancient wood, evoking a sense of age and the passage of time.

As we ventured even deeper into the haunted forest, a greater sense of unease settled in my bones. The forest had a way of making time stand still, as if it existed outside the boundaries of the ordinary world. It felt like a place where the living and the spectral coexisted, their presence intermingling in an uneasy harmony.

This haunted forest held me in its grip, enveloping me in its eerie beauty and unsettling charm.

"I'm not loving this place," I squeaked, ready to make a run for it at any time.

"Faith, mo shíorghra, there's nothing within our territory that would bleeding harm you, and beyond it, there's no damn place where I wouldn't protect you from danger," Rígán declared with a beaming smile.

"Have we let her slip away once more?" Aengus Óg interrupted with a wry smile. "I must admit, my dearest companion, your lack of skill in locating mo sméar iúr has wearied me so."

"Well, she's still here, though that's pretty much all I have to say about it," Rígán exhaled in exasperation before casually leaning against a neighboring tree.

"Truly, my dearest companion, I have grown weary of this ceaseless game of hide and seek," Aengus Óg lamented in a tone reminiscent of a child. "If need be, I shall implore my father to level an cathair ghríobháin, that I may once again be in the presence of mo sméar iúr."

Rígán growled and I was worried he was going to throw some sort of fit. Aengus Óg was clearly not as threatening as an Dagda or Boann, but he was still powerful in his own right and through familial relationships. Their fighting wouldn't help anyone.

"Maybe I could look for her without you two?" I suggested, attempting to deescalate the situation. "She's been willing to meet with me several times in the past."

"No," Rígán spat out before pausing to collect himself. "I absolutely insist, mo bhuanghrá, that you fecking never find yourself in the company of any damn deity, no matter how capable you may be."

"I openly confess that weariness weighs upon me, and respite is required," Aengus Óg conceded. "May I beseech you and my dearest companion to employ your powers of persuasion upon mo sméar iúr and safely escort her back to the castle on my behalf?"

Without waiting for an answer, Aengus Óg startlingly vanished. I was never going to get used to people flitting in and out of a place with no warning. Rígán was clearly not as easily surprised, as he barely acknowledged Aengus Óg's disappearance.

"Do you think she'll come out with you here?" I asked, worried we were about to fail in our task.

"We can only hope," he drawled, hoisting himself off the tree and sauntering towards me. "Surely she knows her damn visit has come to an end. Aengus Óg won't tolerate her presence any longer, mo bhuanghrá, and so neither can I."

"Well, this all hardly seems fair to Caer," I complained, more than ready to take the side of the only person I felt had shown an interest in knowing me as a person. "Shouldn't she get to decide when or if she goes back to him?"

"Surely, she shouldn't have fecking chosen him if she didn't want to be by his side forever," he sneered, lowering his face towards mine. "It seems you don't value vows as much as I do."

"Gods, you're infuriating," I snapped, backing away from him. "Firstly, I absolutely do care about promises, for your information. I just don't think anyone should be held to something they agreed to hundreds of years ago or under duress or without knowing the whole picture! It's complete absurdity for you to say she should have to stay the same for all time or know in one moment how she might feel years later or that she has to hold up her end if he's not holding up his."

"Ah, so everything's fecking contextual and conditional, mo shíorghra?" he countered, moving closer to me.

"Well, yeah actually." I argued, continuing to back away from him. "Sure, we should all strive to make vows in good faith and do our best to keep them. But not over doing what is right for the situation or ourselves if the context changes in a way we couldn't predict or if we're the only one putting in the effort to stay true to the intent of the promise.

For example, my understanding is that Aengus Óg was supposed to be alright with Caer leaving to spend time the way she saw fit; but he has spent hundreds of years not holding up that end of the deal. So, what, now she's the bad guy because, for once, she's holding him accountable for his shit and taking control of her own situation as she was promised she would be able to do in the beginning?"

"You make such an eloquent argument, mo bhuanghrá," he praised me, attempting to trap me against a nearby tree, "But none of your words take into account our bleeding culture, hierarchy, or the power dynamics at play. You speak as if you know what's right, but you can only see it from your own damn perspective."

"Look, I don't like it, but you're not wrong," I admitted, slipping away from his advances. "But that doesn't mean I'm entirely or even partially wrong. Just because something has been a certain way forever or is accepted as the norm, does not actually make it right. I can't change, though I would like to try, what the beings of Tír na nÓg have believed in or chosen to follow as their way of life, but I can support a friend that is doing something that seems right to me."

"It seems like a futile and exhausting effort to fight against the damn inevitable," he drawled, still invading my personal space.

"Good to know," I quipped and rolled my eyes. "So, tell me, what should she have done to make Aengus Óg hold up his side of their agreement, not that I am saying I even believe he should have had that power over her autonomy to begin with, when it became apparent that he only cared about his end being upheld?"

Rígán stopped moving and seemed to be considering his words carefully.

I scooted further away, giving myself some breathing room from his heady presence. It was difficult to argue with him when his proximity made me want to focus on more carnal interactions.

"I must admit, I don't have the answer," he finally confessed after a long pause. "She couldn't seek justice from an Dagda, an Morrígan, or Bobd Derg. Boann wouldn't likely understand her situation, let alone support her damn cause. She lacks the power to defy him alone and wouldn't bleeding likely find allies. She's done all she could in this situation without making it utter shite for herself. Unfortunately, even that rebellion must come to an damn end."

I was filled with a sense of warmth at his words. He had truly been listening and considering what I was telling him. Again, we were talking bare minimums for a real relationship here, but it felt like real progress.

"I don't want to be a part of upholding something I don't believe in," I said and took a step towards him.

Chapter Fifteen

~ Rígán ~

And wouldn't you fecking believe it, Caer Ibormeith just casually strolled right out of the forest, as if she appeared outta thin air, leaving poor Moira gasping for air. Turns out, she had been eavesdropping on us since we arrived, but at least we don't have to go searching for her now. Even though nothing in this place could harm us, the atmosphere still gave me the creeps.

"Caer, I'm so sorry about everything," Moira said with genuine concern. "I really don't want to be a part of any of this and I tried to get everyone to leave you alone."

"Ah, my dear friend, I've known from the start that you were a loyal soul," Caer Ibormeith replied, pulling Moira into a tight embrace. "Rígán spoke true, and I can no longer bear the burden of concealment, for it endangers us both.

The time has come to confront my beloved and lay everything bare."

"What will you do?" Moira asked, her face filled with worry. "Can I help in any way?"

"My dear friend, you're an absolute gem," Caer Ibormeith reassured her, with an enigmatic air. "You have gone above and beyond, surpassing all others in your tireless efforts on my behalf. Your kindness knows no limits."

It was obvious that Moira wasn't too thrilled about that. It broke my heart to see her in such a state. For some fecking reason, she thought sticking her nose in the business of the damn Túatha Dé Danann would lead to a happy ending.

"Let's head back to the castle, Aengus Óg is waiting for us," I declared, eager to be done with all this commotion.

"Surely, you can sense the yearning within me to walk this path back myself," Caer Ibormeith insisted. "If these moments are to be my last taste of unbound freedom for who knows how long, I desire to savor them while I still possess the chance."

I couldn't argue with the goddess of sleep, dreams, and prophecy. As long as she eventually made it back to the castle, Aengus Óg could handle the slight delay. Besides, Moira seemed thrilled to bits with Caer Ibormeith's company.

"Moira and I shall join you on the stroll back," I told her, basking in Moira's approving grin. "With my direction, an cathair ghríobháin won't be an issue."

~ Moira ~

I accepted Rígán's proffered hand and we left the haunted forest for the towering hedged corridors of an cathair ghríobháin.

Everything felt safer with Rígán around and Caer's presence always put me at ease. I could almost believe everything was going to be alright.

The maze was insanely complicated and daunting. Yet, Rígán strode confidently through the twists and turns, a glint of pride in his eyes, as he showed us all the hidden and most direct paths to the castle. Every time we arrived at a dead end or walls that seemed impossible to navigate, he easily guided us through each obstacle.

We passed by different areas of the maze, each with its own unique landscape and atmosphere. The mountain section, in particular, stood out to me, with its towering peaks and rugged terrain. I couldn't wrap my mind around how I could see such a massive feature within that region of the maze, but not when I wasn't within that area itself.

Too often I felt like I had to just accept something and chalk it up to magic, it made me long for scientific and logical explanations.

I peeked into another area of an cathair ghríobháin, as we were passing it, and a vast seascape unfurled before my eyes, with sand and water stretching as far as my vision could reach. The symphony of crashing waves reverberated through the air, creating a soothing rhythm that harmonized with the gentle breeze. The salty tang of the sea air tickled my senses, invigorating my spirit and beckoning me to find solace along the shore.

I yearned to immerse myself in this coastal paradise, to feel the cool sand beneath my feet and let the ocean's embrace wash away the cares of the world. Stepping onto the shore, I was sure the fine grains of sand would welcome me with their warmth, caressing my skin and leaving a trail of footprints as I ventured further.

Gazing out over the expansive waters, I was captivated by the ever-changing hues that danced upon the surface. The sun's rays transformed the sea into a kaleidoscope of colors—a tapestry of azure, turquoise, and hints of emerald and sapphire. The sunlight wove a radiant pathway upon the water, a celestial invitation to venture into the unknown.

Even from where I stood at the entrance, I could see that in the distance, small islands emerged like emerald gems on the horizon, their green foliage contrasting against the vastness of the sea. They held a magnetic allure, hinting at hidden coves and secret havens yet to be discovered. Graceful seabirds soared above the water, their wings outstretched as they rode the gentle currents, adding a soothing touch to the natural beauty that embraced the seascape.

As I stood there, enveloped in the tranquil atmosphere, a sense of serenity washed over me. The world seemed to pause, allowing me to embrace the sheer majesty of this

coastal realm. It was a sanctuary for the weary soul, a haven where time slowed down, and worries were swept away with the ebbing tide. How I longed to linger on the shore, to listen to the symphony of crashing waves, and to witness the ever-changing dance of light upon the sea.

"Hey, do you guys' mind if we take a quick break?" I asked maybe a little too eagerly. "I swear the water is calling to me."

"Ah, you're spot on, mo shíorghra," Rígán drawled with a smirk. "What's the bleeding point of a maze if there aren't temptations trying to lure you astray?"

"I wouldn't mind resting," Caer announced and walked towards the beach.

"I've got something to show you, mo bhuanghrá," Rígán said as he pulled me towards the shoreline.

I let out a gasp and my eyes widened in amazement at the incredible sight before me. Just a week ago, I would have thought myself insane if I had come across a scene like this. The creatures that frolicked and danced in the waves were unlike anything I had ever seen before.

The mermaids, with their shimmering green hair and tails, sang hauntingly beautiful songs that held me spellbound. What fascinated me even more was the strange headgear they wore on top of their heads, which resembled a cocked hat. As I listened to their otherworldly music, a sense of enchantment washed over me.

Dark movement in the water caught my eye. As my gaze shifted towards the massive otter-like creatures with razor-sharp teeth, I felt a twinge of fear run through me. Their sleek black fur and predatory movements were both beautiful and terrifying.

Then I saw the massive sea serpents with their shimmering scales and silent movements gliding through the depths of the water. They were both majestic and menacing, and I couldn't help but feel a sense of awe mixed with terror as I watched them move. Yet, I couldn't help but be captivated by their beauty.

"The merrow, dobhar-chú, and oilliphéist love to visit or make their homes here," he explained as if that meant

anything to me. "An cathair ghríobháin is like a haven for many of the Aes Sídhe."

"I'm at a loss," I confessed, completely enchanted. "Can you tell me more about them?"

"Surely you've heard of the oilliphéist, the sea serpent-like creatures that dwell in our lakes and rivers?" he enthused with great delight, and I enjoyed how he came alive as he described the inhabitants of an cathair ghríobháin. "They've been the stuff of heroic tales for bleeding generations! While the Loch Ness Monster might be the most famous of them now, none can match the infamy of Caoránach, who claimed to be the damn mother

of demons. After she devoured all the land's cattle, a hero named Conan or some shite, ironically blamed for her existence, stuck a sword in her gob and defeated her. Lough Dearg got its name from the blood that flowed from her dying body, staining the rocks a deep red."

I hung on to his every word.

"The dobhar-chú, you see, they live in the waters and have fur with protective qualities," he exclaimed with great enthusiasm. "They're mighty reclusive and rarely venture out of Tír na nÓg, so most humans haven't got a fecking clue about them. Despite being damn near five times bigger than

your average otter and looking quite intimidating, their temperament is still pretty much like an otter's."

"I never would have guessed that," I chuckled. "They look so fierce!"

"Ah, them merrow-maidens, you might know them as sirens, sea-nymphs, or mermaids," he said with a shrug and a grin. "As you can see from here, they're like a lovely lass from the waist up, and fecking fishy below, with greenish scales on their tails. They all have green hair and a wee bit of webbing between their fingers. The merrow-maidens are generally sweet and kind-hearted creatures, often falling for humans. They might live with their human lovers on land or entice them down into the waves, where the men live bleeding enchanted lives.

The little ones born from a merrow and a human mostly look human, but they have scaly skin and membranes between their fingers and toes. But all merrow need a magical cap, a cohuleen druith, like the ones they're wearing there, to travel between the deep waters and dry land. A merrow who's been living on land will almost always go back to the sea, their instincts are too bleeding strong to resist. But if their earthly family hides their cohuleen druith from them, they'll be stuck on land until they find it.

Now, you might wonder why the merrow-maidens go after human men, but that's because the males of their species are quite the damn sight. There aren't any around here right now, but they've got green hair and teeth, piggy eyes, a red nose, a tail between their scaly legs, and stubby fin-like arms. They hardly ever leave the deep waters, but they've been known to snatch the souls of drowned sailors and lock them up in cages under the sea."

"I honestly don't know what to say," I said wistfully, taking in all the information and trying to process it. "Tír na nÓg, an cathair ghríobháin, and everything I've seen so far are all so incredibly beautiful, even though there are moments when I'm terrified by it all."

"Ah, you've hit the fecking nail on the head, mo shíorghra," he drawled, pulling me in closer. "Our world, and sure it's your world too, is a dangerous yet bleeding magnificent place. But you needn't worry yourself too much, for I'll keep you safe from any damn horrors. It's all about strength and power here, it's what decides one's fate, after all."

"You were quite cute just now, all animated and invested in your explanations," I mumbled, not quite sure how to compliment him.

Rígán blushed. I don't think I'd ever seen him blush before and I could feel his delight pulse between us. If I stared at him any longer it would become awkward for us both.

"Why do they stay here instead of out in Tír na nÓg?" I wondered out loud.

"Aye, they're safe and sound in this place," he boasted with a hint of smugness. "A good number of them wouldn't have the fecking guts or the courage to survive in the outside world. An cathair ghríobháin shields them from any gobshites who'd dare take advantage of them or force them to go against their natural ways of living."

"Why?" I asked incredulously.

"Cause I've gone through all the trouble to make it that way," he huffed.

"But, why?" I probed, his answer made no sense in relation to everything he'd said and I'd seen about Tír na nÓg.

"Aye, it's not worth digging into," he murmured, tugging me towards Caer. "But let it be known that the king before me was a bit of a bleeding tyrant, and my early days here were far from easy. That's why I yearned for a sanctuary where others could thrive and live in peace, without a hint of dread."

I let that soak in. There was so much about Rígán and this world that I didn't know or understand. I needed to start asking more questions.

Caer had made herself comfortable on a blanket in the grass near the sandy shoreline. Her smile seemed forced as she watched us approach. My heart went out to her, I hated what she was being forced to go through.

"Hey," I greeted her. "Mind if we join you?"

"Ah, but of course not, my dear friend," she reassured me and patted the space on the blanket next to her. "You are forever welcome to join me."

Rígán and I joined her and made ourselves comfortable. Someone magicked a delightful charcuterie of cured meats, cheeses, and gourmet accompaniments, and we ate in contemplative silence. It would be all too easy to get used to this type of luxury and forget to care about anything else.

~ Rígán ~

Back in the hedges of an cathair ghríobháin, I decided to take a wee detour to put an extra spring in Moira's step.

Now, I knew that the neighboring bogland wasn't exactly a splendid place to hang about, but for some reason, they decided to lay low there. If it was any other spot, I wouldn't have suspected a bleeding thing, but why else would they be spending time in a fecking bog?

"Let's make a quick stop in here," I suggested to Moira and Caer Ibormeith, motioning towards the bog.

"Really?" Moira groaned, scrunching up her face as the foul stench hit her nose.

It was a smell that could knock a person off their feet, a potent reminder of the organic decay that defined the bog's ecosystem.

Caer Ibormeith, bless her soul, didn't complain and just went on ahead.

Moira followed suit, moving more carefully, sticking to the solid ground. It was quite a sight to see her delicate side, a far cry from her feisty nature.

The atmosphere in the bog weighed down on me like a suffocating blanket, heavy and muggy. Every step I took sunk into the soft and squishy ground, as if it were trying to devour me. The bog was a treacherous wasteland, where finding solid footing was like striking gold.

As I surveyed the marshlands, it was an endless expanse of murky greens, blending together like a nightmare. Patches of heather and bog cotton scattered across the land, injecting specks of color into the monotonous palette. The waters that slithered through the bog appeared dark and foreboding, their depths seeming bottomless. The stillness of the water reflected the twisted branches hanging above, creating an eerie mirage and adding to the unsettling ambiance that pervaded the place.

In the distance, the calls of unseen birds echoed through the air, their haunting cries carried by the damp breeze. Every now and then, the silence was broken by the croaking of frogs, their voices reverberating across the marshlands in an eerie chorus. It was a symphony of nature's hidden residents, a reminder that life persisted even in the harshest and most unwelcoming environments.

Within this desolate landscape, a delicate balance existed between life and decay, a damn testament to the sheer resilience and adaptability of nature itself. To be honest, the bog was not my idea of a jolly time. Sure, I may have conjured it into existence, but that didn't mean I enjoyed being stuck in it.

"Come on out now," I roared, all full of beans. "I know you're here, just itching to catch a glimpse of her."

"Mo rí[83]… and a stór!" Senán shouted. "We've been dreadfully concerned about you. Are you feeling grand?"

Sure, Senán was riding Maelgwn, splashing through the bog like a fecking mad lad, water flying everywhere. Ruairidh was scampering after him, like a dog chasing a bleeding stick, and he could've caught up if he went on all fours. Eald was lagging behind them, looking like he wasn't too sure about showing his face to me.

"Gods, it's good to see you all," Moira gasped as she clocked them.

"Sorcha!" roared Ruairidh, spotting her next to me, and he dashed ahead like a bleeding greyhound.

"Sure, it's Moi…" I started to say, but Moira shushed me with a wave.

Ruairidh charged towards her like a madman and gave her a big squeeze, which she returned with a joyful laugh.

Even though tears welled up in her eyes, her smile was radiant. I couldn't understand why these púcaí meant so much to her, considering she hadn't spent much time with them, but it was clear as day that they did.

----

[83] Mo rí (moh ree): My king.

"How have you guys been?" she asked, still holding Ruairidh tightly. "I'm sorry I haven't been able to check in before now."

"We're grand, a stór, but it's yourself that we've been mighty worried about!" Senán exclaimed, shooting me a sideways glance that I wouldn't typically tolerate.

"Cor blimey, I've been goin' on at Dunstan about ya, but the geezer's been as silent as a bloody graveyard," Eald grumbled, pointedly avoiding eye contact. "All 'e said was you're sound and we should just get on with it."

"I'm sorry that I've caused you so much trouble and worry," Moira sniffled, visibly upset. "I really am just fine and appreciate you all so much more than I could ever say."

"Surely, would it not be a grand idea to bring them to the castle in our company?" Caer Ibormeith suggested, much to my annoyance.

"Aye, fecking come along," I groaned, trying to hide my irritation. "I'm sure your new queen would be chuffed to have you as guests."

"Your Majesty?" Senán gasped, bowing as deeply as possible while sitting on Maelgwn. "Mo bhanríon[84], you should have informed us immediately!"

I let out a chuckle at the mere thought of his swift obedience. I remembered when I made Senán, about two and a half centuries ago, using some noble's bastard child

---

[84] Mo bhanríon (moh van-ree-uhn): My queen.

that they wanted to keep hidden. In my opinion, he always had a bleeding peculiar attachment to that truth.

"Ope, well…" Moira stuttered, her words faltering.

"We gotta go," I said firmly, pulling Moira along and not bothering to check who was following us. "If you want to come along, then bleeding tag along."

Moira took my hand and smiled up at me, genuine happiness flowing through our connection, while Ruairidh held her other hand. She seemed overly grateful for such a small gesture, but it still warmed my heart to be a part of it.

Chapter Sixteen

~ Moira ~

"It's an absolute privilege to be in the company of the Goddess of slumber, visions, and divination," Senán professed staring admiringly up at Caer. "Not in all my days did I dare to dream of such a rare delight as this."

Caer murmured in gratitude, "I am deeply obliged."

"I hope it's not rude to ask, but what does he mean by Goddess of sleep, dreams, and prophecy?" I asked hesitantly, not wanting to offend but deeply curious.

"Ah, now that is a question shrouded in secrets, my dear. What, indeed." Caer's response was laced with a hint of intrigue, and with a sly wink, she left me pondering in bewilderment.

"Sorry if I overstepped," I interrupted, now embarrassed I had asked at all.

"Ah, worry not, my dear friend," Caer replied, her smile enigmatic. "I hold the sacred sight, bestowing upon me the power to unveil prophetic visions to those who seek my guidance. I am the shepherd of mortal souls in the realm of dreams, aiding them in deciphering the veiled depths of their subconscious. Alas, scarce are the seekers of my aid in these modern days."

"So, you could tell me my future?" I asked incredulously.

"Nay, my powers cannot penetrate the veils that shroud the Aes Sídhe and Túatha Dé Danann." Caer's laughter tinkled like chimes in the wind. "It is only the lives of mortals that I can illuminate with my gifts."

"Would you be able to tell me about Baz and Lex's futures?" I whispered, not sure which answer would be more painful.

"Aye," Caer let out a deep sigh before continuing, her voice laced with mystery. ""I could reveal the multitude of paths that lie ahead, and which ones are most likely to unfold. However, what you may hear may not be to your desire. Nor can I assure you a means to alter the outcome. So, I pose this question: Do you still yearn to know?"

"Yes, please tell me," I insisted, given the option I would always choose knowing something over not, even if it was the more painful route.

"You dead set, mo bhuanghrá?" Rígán interrupted, his voice laced with caution. "Them visions from Caer

Ibormeith aren't exactly a walk in the park, life's a fecking struggle enough as it is."

"Yes, I'm sure," I confirmed, even though I wasn't.

"Very well, my dear friend, then I shall divulge what I perceive, but do inform me if you wish me to cease at any moment," Caer whispered softly, her gaze fixed upon the distance. "I behold three potential futures for them, equally probable and shrouded in uncertainty. In one of these, they shall eventually emerge from the cloak of mourning for your departure and embark upon a life brimming with joy and purpose. They shall flourish in their vocations, deepen their emotional ties, and extend their aid to those marginalized. They may even embrace a child and nourish it with boundless love. Such is the existence they both yearn for.

In the second future, they shall fail to surmount their sorrow and remain ensnared in its clutches. Despite their valiant efforts, they shall be unable to cast off the weight of their grief and gradually descend into a realm of profound desolation. Their once-beautiful dwelling shall wither into an empty husk, teeming with memories that only intensify their anguish. Their careers shall falter as they grapple with their sorrow, and they shall grow increasingly detached from the world around them. They shall be trapped in an unending cycle of sorrow, devoid of any glimmer of happiness. This destiny serves as a dire reminder of the catastrophic toll grief can exact upon even the mightiest of souls.

The third future is less defined, yet equally likely to the ones preceding it. It commences in the same manner as the second, with them ensnared in their grief. However, they shall be visited by a Bean Sí and Túatha Dé Danann, who shall present them with a path to Tír na nÓg. After accepting this offer, I cannot foresee how their fate shall unfold."

"Fuck," I muttered, crestfallen there was no clear way to guarantee their well-being.

"Aye, fuck indeed," Caer muttered, her face grim. "I wish I could provide more solace."

"Ope, Caer, please don't think I'm upset with you in any way!" I hurried to assure her. "I really appreciate that you told me what you could. I know none of this is on you in any way. Being able to see the future doesn't mean you set it in motion or control it."

"Truly, my dear friend, you are indeed a most thoughtful companion," Caer chuckled dryly.

Rígán squeezed my hand and I could feel him trying to soothe me through our bond.

I gripped his hand in return and gave him a watery smile. I appreciated his attempt to console me and, in the future, I hoped he would offer me his thoughts on what he would do if he were in my shoes.

~ Rígán ~

I was getting sick of sharing Moira's time with people I couldn't give a toss about. It might upset Caer Ibormeith, but it was time to make our way to the castle and get everyone the hell outta there. I made a beeline for the edge of Púcaí City and rushed everyone along.

Finally, we managed to escape the twists and turns of an cathair ghríobháin and stepped into the open air of late afternoon. And there it was, the sight of the wall surrounding my city.

The gate and walls outside my city were massive and intimidating, towering up into the sky like a warning to anyone foolish enough to come close. The design was meant to be chaotic and frightening, meant to put the fear of God into any intruders.

Despite the frightening atmosphere, I felt a surge of pride course through me as we approached the gates. This was my city, and I was its king. While the walls and faces were designed to scare off invaders, they also served as a testament to the strength and power of my kingdom.

"Open the bleeding gates!" I barked before those useless guards caught us slipping. They were too relaxed at their posts, the gobshites.

As they clapped eyes on me, they scrambled to do as I commanded and we legged it into the city.

We strolled through Púcaí City, taking in the flashy colors and the busy vibe of my kingdom. The púcaí were all about their business, buying and selling, going about their lives. They all greeted us with deep bows, flashy waves, and wide grins.

I sneaked a glance at Moira to see how she was reacting, and I was chuffed to see the awe and affection in her eyes. I grinned to myself as we wandered through, taking in the sights and sounds of my home. There truly was no place like it in all the land.

As we made our way up the steep hill to my castle in the heart of the city, I couldn't help but feel proud and satisfied.

"Pray, do inform my beloved that he may come across me at the lake beyond the castle walls," Caer Ibormeith declared and poofed away.

"These damn Túatha Dé Danann are a fecking delight," I grumbled and rolled my eyes. "No need to climb those bleeding stairs if that's the case."

I whisked us all to the throne room and had a good laugh secretly at their gasps when we arrived. Aengus Óg was lounging on my bleeding throne, pretending to take a nap.

"You know where she is," I barked, not interested in pleasantries or chit-chat.

"Ah, my dearest companion, a ray of sunshine you are," Aengus Óg taunted, opening one eye. "Once I grasp mo sméar iúr, so rare and bright, we shall celebrate in bliss, with you and Moira, fair and right, and your 'enchanting comrades', a troupe of exquisite might."

And with that, he disappeared, leaving the throne room feeling less stuffy. Now, the only thing left to do was to ditch those 'charming companions' so that Moira and I could enjoy some alone time. But the problem was, she'd probably want to keep them around.

"Mo shíorghra, it's already late in the day and I could use a bit of relaxation before Aengus Óg comes back," I said, using my most charming tone. "Let me sort your mates out with some rooms so they can chill and freshen up for the big feast we'll be having tonight. You might want to join me in doing the same."

"Ah, that might be nice, I am a bit grungy from walking all day," she pondered, glancing over at her mates for agreement. "What do you guys want to do? I can stay here and catch up with you if you'd prefer?"

"Mo bhanríon, you simply must prioritize your regal duties over engaging in conversation with us!" Senán interrupted, shocked at the idea of her doing anything else, and I couldn't help but appreciate his posh manners for once. "Naturally, we too must prepare ourselves for this most auspicious occasion. Can you imagine, tonight we shall be dining with some of the most eminent and influential members of the Túatha Dé Danann. It's almost too good to be true!"

"Sound then, it's sorted," I grunted before anyone could argue. "Dunstan! Come in here and show our 'guests' to their rooms."

"Let's crack on then, yeah?" Dunstan grumbled as he strolled in, him and Teàrlag always lurking about somewhere close by, a trait I highly valued in my generals.

"Aye, I wanna sta' wi' Sorcha!" Ruairidh complained, ruining my perfect plan.

"Oh, quit yer bloody whinging, Ruairidh," Eald mumbled, glancing at me. "Let the king and queen have a bit of time on their own. We'll be seein' them at the feast soon enough. And I heard Dunstan was goin' to sort you out with a bubble bath."

"Oi, I never said that," Dunstan objected before I interrupted him.

"He certainly fecking will!" I exclaimed, grateful to Eald. "He'll also get you some sweets."

"Hey, sweets?" Ruairidh exclaimed hungrily. "Aye, awright. I can hae a wee fizzy bath an' gobble some bonnie treats afore tea wi' Sorcha. But I wanna be sittin' richt beside her!"

"Of course, my dear Ruairidh," Moira happily agreed. "I wouldn't have it any other way."

~ Moira ~

Walking into Rígán's en suite bathroom, I was again struck by its opulence. The walls were intricately decorated with gold leaf accents and plush, velvet drapes. The floor was made of gleaming marble, and the room was lit by the soft glow of candlelight.

To my left, a colossal, claw-footed bathtub beckoned invitingly. It was crafted from polished silver and adorned with filigree that glittered in the flickering light. This time, I took the time to really look at the intricate carvings along its sides. They depicted scenes of fairies and other magical creatures frolicking. I couldn't help but smile at the charming imagery.

It was clear time had been spent making sure the immaculate design of this lavish and enchanting room met his vision.

"Are you coming in?" I asked Rígán who stood at the entrance watching me explore.

"I was fecking waiting for an invite, mo bhuanghrá," he explained with a smirk. "I'm trying hard to not overstep your boundaries today."

"I've noticed," I acknowledged and did my best to push how pleased that made me through our bond.

"Spotted enough for a prize?" he asked, coming close enough that I could feel the heat from his skin on mine.

"Maybe," I teased with a quick smile. "Why don't we take a bath together and see how it goes?"

"I'm damn fond of that idea, mo shíorghra," he drawled, and our clothes disappeared.

By the look of him, he more than just liked the idea. He was already semi-erect and if the desire coming off of him was any indication, it wouldn't take much to get him the rest of the way.

I appreciated the willpower he was exerting to stop his own needs from overriding my own.

"Do you think you could ride the line between genuinely experiencing the depths of your feelings and not forcing me into a trance?" I inquired, hoping he could.

"Sure, I'll give it a lash," he purred, still so close but not yet touching me.

"I think I'd like for you to take the lead," I blurted out before I lost the courage. "But I have to be fully present at all times or I won't want to try again any time soon."

Rígán nodded his assent and his accompanying wicked grin gave me palpitations.

All at once I was in his arms, his lips were slanted over mine, his mouth swallowing my gasp. His fingers were in my curls, I was moaning, his passion mingling with my own, and I couldn't resist the intensity of the moment.

So, I didn't, I let myself fall into him and trusted he would catch me.

Breaking our kiss, he led me to the tub that was already filled with steaming hot water. He easily lifted me into the tub and then joined me. Even with the two of us now sitting in it, the tub could easily hold several more people. He pulled me into his lap facing him and then he was kissing me again, with an intense hunger, pouring all of his emotion into the moment.

I felt both of our bodies slacken, melting into each other in a way I never thought possible. It was as if we were both finally, for the first time, letting our guards down and allowing ourselves to be truly vulnerable in that moment.

We were locked in a deep kiss, that I had to pause occasionally to catch my breath, but I hated each second of being parted from him. Without hesitation, I would jump right back into the fervent embrace as soon as I could.

The passion with which he kissed me was overwhelming, as he devoured my mouth and filled me with intense desire, leaving my lips swollen and clouding my eyes with lust.

On the verge of losing myself to his passion, he pulled back, giving me a moment to collect myself while he nibbled on my neck. As I regained control, he ran his tongue down my chest, mouth latching onto one nipple while his fingers played with the other.

At some point my fingers found their way into his hair and I grasp it tightly as I arch my back and in pleasure.

I ground against his impressive and now fully hard length; it was almost embarrassing how badly I wanted him inside of me. At least it would've been embarrassing if I couldn't feel how much he wanted the same thing.

His hips rut up into me, leaving me panting with need.

I felt him smile as his mouth closed around the opposite nipple, drawing the moment out, ignoring my obvious desires.

Whining but not willing to vocalize my needs, I took what friction I could from writhing against him.

I closed my eyes, groaning as I felt an orgasm building, just as I was about to come his hands held my hips in place, robbing me of it at the last second.

"Gods, why?" I wailed in outrage, opening my eyes to find his staring intently into mine.

"Let me be the one to give you a good time, mo bhuanghrá," he cajoled and I would have laughed if not for the completely serious look on his face. "I promise to fecking outdo whatever you can do on your own, no doubt about it."

"For fucks sake," I huffed in annoyance, aware that his track record on that account spoke volumes. "I'll try, but I'm not making any lifelong promises here."

"Ah, you're fecking flawless like that, all flustered and gasping for it," he crooned into my ear and then I could feel the heat of his gaze as he swept his eyes across my skin, taking me in. "Sure, we were born to be united like this."

His praise made me blush. I loved how sincere he was every time he complimented me. I wasn't quite ready to reciprocate, but a part of me wanted to.

Suddenly, Rígán lifted me onto the edge of the tub and steadied me as he knelt in front of me. He spread my legs apart and leaned closer, his breath teasing my clit.

I moaned as he buried his face between my legs and flicked his tongue over my sensitive flesh. He was carefully sucking and licking, each sensation driving me to delirium. Each touch sent me spiraling toward ecstasy, and when he gently nipped at my clit, I groaned in pleasure.

I knew I was going to come soon if he kept this up.

"I'm getting so close," I rasped, not wanting to tell him.

As he pulled back, a panicked yelp escaped my lips. My hips pushed upwards, searching for the pressure he had abruptly stripped away, leaving me desperate for more. I felt like I might cry.

"Shh, mo shíorghra," Rígán chuckled with a glint in his eye.

My glare held no sway over him as he stood and picked me up off the edge of the tub.

Back into the water, he brought me down onto his lap again. I wiggled against him, choosing to ignore his cross look as well.

I felt his cock become lubricated with something more than just water as I slipped up and down its length.

He smirked before impaling me on it in a perfectly timed thrust.

I howled in surprise as my body fought to adapt to him, pleasure quickly winning out over pain.

"Súnás domsa, mo bhuanghrá,"[85] he grunted between thrusts and my world split open.

I came hard, a frenzied bliss rolling through me.

He continued to fuck me, his cock hitting every sensitive spot, extending my rapture until it bordered on torment.

He kissed me fiercely as he climaxed and I felt complete.

---

[85] Orgasm for me, my love.

Chapter Seventeen

~ Rígán ~

Faith and begorrah, after a fecking grand ride with Moira, the lass was always sound and agreeable, letting me take care of her. I loved giving her a good scrub down and playing with her lovely locks while doing so. It was an intimate experience, no doubt, and one I hadn't quite had the pleasure of before.

Sure, and didn't I sweet-talk her into letting me choose her outfit for the big feast, even though she insisted I spend as much time on myself as I did on her. I thought it'd be a bit boring, like picking out my own clothes every day, but truth be told, it was a bleeding riot blending our styles together. And, of course, I wanted us to make a grand impression, something that'd leave jaws dropping all around.

For myself, I went with a pure white silk tunic, all fancy with gold thread embroideries, and a pair of matching breeches. My cloak, made of the softest velvet in a deep forest green, was held together with a silver bull clasp, a symbol of my power and authority. And my scrying shillelagh seemed like the perfect addition to my ensemble.

As for Moira, I went with a stunning silver gown, so delicate it was practically see-through. The bodice was decorated with intricate patterns of opals and silver thread that sparkled and shimmered with every movement she made. Her hair was done up in curls, flowing down her back, and she topped it all off with a tiara made of diamonds and opals, catching the light and scattering colors all around the room like a proper kaleidoscope.

As we strolled into the grand hall, a fierce sense of pride and pure exhilaration washed over me. My queen, looking resplendent and majestic, sauntered by my side, her hand firmly holding mine. At that moment, we felt like an unstoppable force, like nothing could bleeding touch us.

The grand hall was a sight to behold, decked out with intricate tapestries, fancy candelabras, and flashy statues. Hundreds of candles cast a warm glow, filling the space with a cozy atmosphere, while the mouthwatering aroma of roast meats and baked goodies tantalized my nostrils.

At the far end of the hall, a grand feast was laid out on a long, fancy table. The meats looked absolutely delicious, I knew they'd be cooked to perfection and bursting with flavors, accompanied by a rainbow of vibrant vegetables and fruits. Crystal goblets filled to the brim with the finest wines and meads were placed with great care all around, creating mesmerizing reflections of color on the walls.

Two majestic thrones stood proudly, separate from the long communal table where our guests would be sitting. They were crafted from top-notch materials and adorned with sparkling gemstones. The sight of them only intensified my already palpable excitement for the arrival of our guests, and I knew deep down that this feast would be a unforgettable night for all who were lucky enough to be there.

When we gathered for the feast, Moira would be sitting to my left at the head of the grand table, with her mates taking the seats of honor on her left. To my right, there were seats reserved for Aengus Óg and Caer Ibormeith, likely to pop up when I least fecking expected.

I hated that this whole shindig was for those whimsical and worthless Túatha Dé Danann, but at least it gave me an excuse to entertain Moira. And it was the perfect chance to introduce her to all the púcaí as their queen. I made sure every fecker in the city and an cathair ghríobháin got an invite to join us.

Our guests would be arriving soon, and Dunstan and Teàrlag would be at the castle and hall entrances to greet them and show them to their seats. I pointed Moira to the matching thrones, where we'd be waiting for our esteemed guests to arrive.

She seemed a tad nervous, but I'd be there to make sure it was a perfect night for her.

~ Moira ~

The air was thick with the mouthwatering aroma of roasted meats and freshly baked goods, a tantalizing scent that enveloped my senses. It was clear that no expense had been spared in preparing this feast, and I couldn't help but feel overwhelmed by Rígán's thoughtfulness. My stomach rumbled in response, betraying my growing hunger as I nervously sat upon the throne as Rígán and I awaited our guests.

I could feel my heart racing as they began to arrive, and I wondered if everything was prepared to their liking. It was a bit nerve-wracking to be the center of such grandeur and attention. Nothing in my life had prepared me for this and I was terrified I'd make a fool of myself or Rígán. I had no idea what the customs were here and Rígán had been no help, assuring me that anything I did would be perfect.

Thankfully, the first púcaí I welcomed were Eald, Senán, Ruairidh, and Maelgwn. Ruairidh looked the same as ever and I embraced him before ushering him to his seat. His childlike glee at attending the feast was contagious and I started to look forward to the rest of the night.

Tonight, Eald carried himself with dignity and grace. He was dressed in finery provided by Rígán, wearing a skullcap and breeches that matched the colors of his green tunic. His clothing was adorned with intricate embroidery and tiny jewels that glinted in the light. However, as he approached us, I could see that he was nervous.

"Yer Majesties," he said, bowing before us. "I'm well chuffed to be here at yer shindig."

"It is a pleasure to have you, Eald," I reassured him with a wide smile. "Please, enjoy the food and drink. I hope we have time to speak more later."

With that, Eald straightened up and made his way to his seat at the feast.

Rígán squeezed my hand and looked at me like I was the only person in the room. Maybe tonight wasn't going to be as hard as I'd anticipated.

Next came Senán, amusingly still riding upon Maelgwn. Rígán had provided him with, what I would never describe to him as, an adorable small suit of armor made of the finest materials, and adorned with intricate patterns. Despite his diminutive stature, he exuded an air of authority and confidence as he made his way towards us.

"Mo rí agus mo bhanríon," he said bowing low, a smile on his face that showed off his sharp little teeth. "It is a grand privilege to partake in your sumptuous banquet."

"It is a pleasure to have you, Senán," I told him. "And you too, Maelgwn."

I watched as he rode towards his seat and appraised his placement to my left with pride. It felt good to be able to reward him in a way that meant so much to him for his loyalty and assistance. I wasn't Sorcha, but I would do right by the friends she made.

One by one, the rest of the invited Aes Sídhe arrived in their various forms and colors. Some were elegant and refined, while others were wild and untamed. It was a sight to behold as they entered the grand hall, dressed in their finest clothes, their eyes filled with awe and wonder.

As each guest met me, I greeted them with a smile and a warm welcome, doing my best to make them feel at home. Rígán offered his own kind words, knowing each and every one of them personally. It felt almost too easy to work together with him to make sure each guest was comfortable and well taken care of. Slowly but surely, any concerns I had about the feast melted away.

When I thought everyone had finally arrived, Caer and Aengus Óg appeared before us. They were both resplendent and seemed without a care in the world. I wondered how their talk went and truly hoped Caer was happy with how things played out.

The white gown she wore was a masterpiece of craftsmanship. The fabric was so fine it seemed to float around her, and it was adorned with intricate lace and embroidery. Her long black hair cascaded down her back in loose waves, and she wore a simple silver circlet on her head. The circlet was adorned with delicate crystals that sparkled in the light, adding to the ethereal quality of her appearance.

Aengus Óg' high collared tunic and breeches were no less impressive. The fabric was a rich golden color that seemed to shimmer in the light, and it was embroidered with intricate patterns that seemed to come alive as he moved. His golden curly hair fell in a way that highlighted his chiseled jawline and left his bright blue eyes on full display.

~ Rígán ~

"Ah, sure and you finally made it," I drawled, barely holding back an eye roll. "Welcome, welcome. Have a seat, will you, so we can get on with things."

"Ah, my dearest companion, your hospitality knows no bounds," Aengus Óg teased, in the best form I'd seen him yet. "Mo sméar iúr and I are enraptured to grace your presence this eve."

"My beloved, be reminded that I possess the ability to speak on my own behalf," softly corrected Caer Ibormeith, her smile carrying an enchanting allure capable of penetrating the depths of any soul. "Yet, your words ring true. I find immense delight in the prospect of spending this evening in the company of my dearest friend."

"Right, right," I briskly agreed. "With all due respect, let's have both of you take your seats so we can introduce Moira and get the celebrations rolling."

"With the little respect my dearest companion deems we're deserving of, shall we take our seats, mo sméar iúr?" Aengus Óg crowed in delight.

Caer Ibormeith flashed a charming smile at Moira and gracefully they took their seats, accepting the respect given by the nearby Aes Sídhe. To be honest, they were more agreeable than many of the other damn Túatha Dé Danann.

Holding Moira's hand tight, I braced myself for the speech I'd prepared. There were still matters to be sorted, but Moira was my queen, and everyone had to fecking get that. My heart swelled with pride as I laid eyes on her beauty, grace, and strength. I wouldn't tolerate her being treated anything less than the most precious thing in my realm.

"My esteemed púcaí subjects, along with the grand Túatha Dé Danann, and the rest of the Aes Sídhe gathered around my table," I bellowed, sending a ripple of excitement through the crowd. Waiting for silence to fall, I carried on. "It's with immense pleasure that I introduce to you Moira, mo shíorghra, wife, and your new púcaí queen. She's a woman of immense wisdom, courage, and compassion, and I'm confident she'll be a true leader for our people. I implore you to welcome her with open hearts and open minds, and to treat her with the same love and respect you give me. She's the most precious gem in my kingdom, and I know she'll be the same for all of you. Now, let's cut the yap and start eating, drinking, and, most importantly, celebrating!"

As the crowd exploded in cheers and applause, I grinned at Moira, expressing my love through our connection, and escorted her to our seats at the feast. This was the start of her journey as the púcaí queen, and I longed for it to be a memory brimming with all the joy, beauty, and warmth our kingdom could bestow upon her.

"Thank you," she beamed, and I had never seen her look more glowing, "that was so sweet… I'm kinda at a loss for words. I just really appreciate everything you've done tonight and it's all been so perfect. Thank you."

I knew full well that a whole bunch of my subjects, especially her mates, would be keen to have a chat with her tonight. But it was important that she got a chance to have a feast and relax first. I grasped her hand and guided her to our designated spots at the table. As we settled down, a melodic and captivating melody began to waft through the room.

At the start, it was hardly noticeable, barely catching the attention of those gathered. But as the melody grew in complexity and energy, it became impossible to ignore, filling every nook and cranny of the hall. I had gone for a selection of music that was both ancient and timeless, resonating deep within my very bones. As the melody hung in the air, many of the Aes Sídhe started joining in, adding their own sweet voices to the enchanting tune as they reveled in merrymaking.

Well, then, fecking Boann appeared out of thin air, and the air crackled with an otherworldly tension. I couldn't help but curse my bleeding luck. It felt as if an invisible shroud of fear had descended upon us, causing our guests to stir uneasily in their seats and exchange anxious whispers.

What the feck did she want now? How much longer were these fecking meddling Túatha Dé Danann gonna plague our fecking existence?

From the corner of my eyes, I caught glimpses of movement. The less confrontational and meekest of the Aes Sídhe at the feast were shiteing themselves, terrified of Boann's arrival. Before I could do anything, the fecking cowards had scarpered. Their departure was swift, a testament to their agility and the urgent nature of the situation.

Boann appeared a bit off, maybe even unhinged, in some way. Her magic was snapping chaotically in the air around her like nothing I had ever seen before. I genuinely understood the desire to avoid the fecking drama that was sure to come. Part of me wanted to bugger off from the feast with Moira as well.

However, I didn't have that option and I was furious, itching to do something reckless. The usual caution I had around Boann was overridden by my burning desire to punish anyone who would dare to disturb Moira's night.

"I'm fecking fed up with all of this," I muttered under my breath.

I stood up forcefully, my chair toppled behind me, and readied myself to deal with Boann. This wouldn't be pretty, sure it'd start with talk, but unfortunately, I didn't think it'd stay civil for long. My plans to celebrate Moira had been ruined, and I was ready to do what needed to be done to get the feast back on track, preferably without Boann around.

I paused, taking a moment before stepping towards Boann, as I felt Moira's fear slam through our connection. Glancing her way, I could see her eyes filling with concern and tears.

In my moment of hesitation, I had to give credit to Aengus Óg; he jumped up quick as a flash, after some nudging from Caer Ibormeith, and greeted his dear mother with all the respect she deserved. The rest of the party guests had no choice but to stand up in a show of deference.

As fecking annoying as it was, I was grateful to see Moira's companions and my generals rush to surround her. Not that they would do much against a goddess, but any help protecting Moira was genuinely appreciated and would never be forgotten.

"Mother!" Aengus Óg exclaimed. "What brings you hither? We were just reveling in our fortune. Will you partake in our merriment?"

Caer Ibormeith, with an air of lazy grace, strolled behind Aengus Óg at a leisurely pace to pay her respects to the formidable goddess.

"I've come to ensure that you're tending to everything with your wife, mo mac óg," Boann quipped, jaw clenched and eyes twinkling like stars, she nodded at Aengus Óg before turning to greet Caer Ibormeith. "Ah, it appears you've returned to your rightful place."

I cautiously and ever so slowly circled the table towards Boann's back, aware that I was probably not going unnoticed, but I thought it best not to draw attention to my actions.

"Aye," Caer Ibormeith replied with a smile that held the secrets of ages past. "My beloved and I have settled our affairs. However, it is a fortuitous twist of fate that you have arrived, for we had hoped you could preside over a ritual on our behalf."

"Is that so, mo mac óg?" Boann urged, her brows furrowed, curiosity piqued. "Please do enlighten me."

Boann had yet to outwardly acknowledge my movements, but that didn't mean she was unaware of them.

Nonetheless, something with her did seem amiss, and there was a possibility that she wasn't keeping as close an eye on the situation as she typically would.

"Ah, mother," Aengus Óg cleared his throat, suddenly looking uneasy. "Mo sméar iúr and I have concluded that we shall renew our matrimonial oaths every century or so, commencing posthaste."

"Oh?" Boann questioned with a tone that was too raised to simply indicate her interest. "Why would you want to go through all that trouble? Aren't your current vows sufficient?"

"Nay," Aengus Óg replied with a sigh, shooting Caer Ibormeith a guilty look. "Our current vows do not suffice. Mine yearns for amendment, while mo sméar iúr shall keep hers unchanged."

I was close enough to strike, and a physical attack appeared to be my best chance. But, I couldn't help but wonder what had gotten Boann in such a dreadful state. She was a powerful adversary, no doubt about that, but typically she was much more composed, even when bollocksed.

"I would be most intrigued to hear how yours might differ, mo mac óg," Boann pondered, nearly growling the words. "If I remember correctly, your previous vows were along the lines of 'I commit myself to you, my love, with all that I am and possess. I promise to honor and respect you, to share my joys and sorrows with you, and to stand by your side through all of life's challenges.' Weren't they?"

"What matters is our desire to renew and revisit our vows with each passing century," Aengus Óg ground out with a grin. "We persist in growth and transformation, and thus our binding oaths should follow suit."

I was cautious, for Aengus Óg hadn't made Boann aware of my presence nor intervened in any manner to halt my advance. He either was entirely unconcerned or a fool.

"I see," Boann remarked, even though it was evident by the tone of her voice that she did not. "If this is truly what brings you happiness, mo mac óg, I will always support your joy."

Aengus Óg stretched out his hands towards his mother and drew her into a firm embrace.

"Indeed, mother," Aengus Óg affirmed, while keeping her in a tight embrace. "In truth, swift triumph brings solace fair, I have ventured forth, our quest to speed, my heart does yearn, with haste to proceed. For in its swift fulfillment, my soul does find, a soothing ointment, to calm the mind. With swiftness and purpose, worries shall wane, a tranquil liberation, the spirit shall gain."

With a gesture from him, Caer Ibormeith joined them and rested her hand on Boann's back. I had never witnessed Caer Ibormeith employing such a great deal of her enchantment to soothe another, or to tell the truth, any Túatha Dé Danann before. It was evident that there was some sort of transformation in Boann as a result of this interaction. She appeared considerably more tranquil and had regained her customary composure.

If I had to fight, there was no fecking chance that the other Túatha Dé Danann would lend me a hand. In fact, they'd probably side with her, seeing as they were related and all.

The atmosphere thickened with Boann's sorcery, her power radiating as she worked her magic to transform my grand hall into a fecking wedding wonderland. Snow-white flowers cascaded from every bleeding corner, their petals as pure as the driven snow, giving the hall an ethereal glow. The walls shimmered with delicate lace hanging's and the ceiling was draped in billowing silk, like a canopy of fecking dreams hovering above us.

Boann's sorcery had transformed the grand hall into a vision of splendor, a sight that would be etched into the memories of all who beheld it. The sheer beauty and intricate details spoke of her immense talent and devotion to making this day truly magical.

I couldn't help but roll my eyes at the whole spectacle. The last thing I wanted was to be forced into attending a wedding, especially one presided over by the goddess herself. And what made it worse was that it stole all of Moira's limelight and honor from her big night.

"Rígán, love, sit with me," Moira called out; urgency and hope emanating from her. "I'm honored to be able to witness my friend's re-commitment ceremony."

Both Boann and I turned to look at her, but Boann's attention quickly turned to me.

"Please," Moira begged as she stood, holding her hand out to me.

I would never decline Moira's outstretched hand. Reluctantly, I watched as Aengus Óg tied the knot with Caer Ibormeith.

Aengus Óg's vows were pretty modern, refreshing with their declarations of love, respect, support, and fidelity, and a promise to let his wife make her own decisions. For at least the next hundred years, Caer Ibormeith would be free to wander in any form she pleased without facing any consequences from her hubby or his clan.

I glanced at Moira, trying not to burst out laughing as she got all teary-eyed listening to Aengus Óg's words. Clearly, she didn't know that his vows were straight-up provided by Caer Ibormeith. I gotta hand it to her though, Caer Ibormeith was smart in the vows she wrote, with a modern touch that screamed Moira.

On the other hand, Caer Ibormeith's vows were more like those ancient Celtic marriages. She talked about a bond that surpassed time and space, a commitment to stick by each other through thick and thin, and a promise to be faithful till the end of days.

I reckon Aengus Óg was missing her something fierce, and he might be a right eejit, if this was all he managed to get in return for his vows.

Moira was over the moon for her friend, crying her eyes out watching the love between Aengus Óg and Caer Ibormeith.

Despite my annoyance, I couldn't help but feel a tiny bit moved by the ceremony. There was something truly magical about seeing two people pledging their love and devotion to each other in such a deep and meaningful way. As they sealed their vows with a kiss, I felt a glimmer of hope and optimism for their future together.

If they could work through their differences, surely Moira and I could do it. After all, I was a catch far better than Aengus Óg, and no one, not even a damn goddess, could match up to mo bhuanghrá.

Chapter Eighteen

~ Moira ~

I woke naked in Rígán's arms feeling well rested and content. The night had gone extremely well, especially considering Boann's impromptu visit. After the informal vow renewal, Boann had left and the celebrations had restarted with somehow even more enthusiasm.

Caer had confided in me that she'd spent centuries thinking about the vows she wished Aengus Óg would have been held to, instead of the ambiguous ones he'd easily found ways to not uphold the spirit of. She'd just not been sure exactly how to phrase them or convince Aengus Óg of their veracity until recently. I hoped things between them went well, they seemed to genuinely care for each other.

As I reflected on Aengus Óg and Caer's struggle to maintain their relationship, my own situation with Rígán came to mind. Despite my reservations and his wrongdoings, I couldn't resist my longing for his attention, touch, and wit; just all of him in general.

Of course, I knew that he had to earn my trust and love, but in the meantime, I wouldn't turn down any consensual affection between us. Perhaps I was still clinging to my mortal need for logic, but I couldn't bring myself to succumb to a magical soul bond just because it existed. Whether this inclination would change as I adjusted to living in Tír na nÓg, only time would tell.

Nonetheless, someone wiser than me once said, "If someone's actions consistently demonstrate their true character, trust what they reveal about themselves." So, until I found a more effective approach, I would have to take each day as it came and scrutinize his behavior as he showed me who he truly was.

Resolved to start the day on a high note and leave further musings until another time, I wriggled out of Rígán's embrace. Glancing down, I saw an undeniable bulge in the sheets and his morning wood called to me, heating my core in the most delicious way.

I slipped under the covers, grabbing hold of his cock, feeling its length and girth in my hand. Slowly, I began to stroke him, feeling his dick grow impossibly even harder.

He moaned softly in his sleep and it didn't take long before his cock was fully erect, standing ever so tall and proud.

I repositioned myself so I could grip his thighs as I slipped just the tip into my mouth, using my tongue to swirl the precum as I lazily licked and sucked.

"Fecking hell, you're gonna be the fecking death of me," Rígán groaned as he woke, yanking the sheets away to revel in the full extent of my ministrations.

I looked up at him, humming as I gradually took in as much of his cock as I could on the first go.

I was rewarded for my efforts with a full body shiver as he gasped my name. I could feel myself growing even more wet as Rígán's desire flooded through me.

Still in control, I licked him from root to tip, making sure his cock was completely slick. Working his length in up-and-down and corkscrew motions with my hands, I enthusiastically focused on the tip, teasing and swirling until he was tightly gripping the sheets.

Then, taking his cock in deeply, I set a consistent pace of bobbing and sucking, occasionally using my tongue to flick over his most sensitive spots until he was doing his best to not thrust up into my mouth.

"I'm yearning to be inside you," he growled, pulling me off of him.

"If you insist, love," I rasped in what I hoped was a seductive tone.

"Assume the position on your hands and knees, mo shíorghra," he demanded and then added, "If it fecking pleases you."

I obeyed, more than eager to be fucked by him. Our intermingled passion was pushing at my limits, but he seemed to know just when to pull back on his to allow me to stay present. It was a heady and addictive feeling, even when I was fully aware of what was happening.

Rígán lined himself up behind me, leaning over to kiss a trail down my back before slipping a finger into my already wet core.

"I'm positively enamored with discovering you already slick and eager," he groaned, pushing in a second finger. "Is all this fecking for me then?"

"Gods, yes," I mewled as I shamelessly fucked his hand, core tightening and thighs already beginning to tremble.

"By all means, do not reach your damn peak until I grant the permission," he snarled in warning, bending to nip at my shoulder.

"Gods, you're a fucking monster," I complained but we both knew I would comply with his request.

I could imagine his smirk as I heard him chuckle, withdrawing his fingers.

Before I could gripe about the loss, he was pushing into me, filling me with a breathtaking stretch. Moaning I pushed back into him, wanting everything he could give me.

We were both panting, struggling to keep up with his demanding pace. Each pistoning thrust added to the wonderful pressure building inside me, and I knew I was just seconds away from experiencing pure bliss.

Incoherently, I tried to warn him and was near sobbing when he pulled out.

"I fancy laying eyes on you when you come," he gruffly clarified, flipping me over and easily sliding back in.

I reached up for him and pulled him down onto me, kissing him passionately. My fingers ran through his hair and down his neck, doing anything to draw him closer. Digging my heels into his back, I pressed myself as fully against him as I could manage.

"Come on, indulge in the pure bliss, mo bhuanghrá," Rígán ordered as he broke our kiss to prop himself up on his elbows, allowing his dick to hit me in just the right spot.

I sobbed through the blinding orgasm, disjointedly chanting his name as he watched me and drew out my pleasure with expert strokes on my clit. My body was wracked with pleasure, and I could feel wave after wave of orgasmic bliss coursing through me.

Fucking Rígán was likely as close to experiencing nirvana as a person could get. He may not have been a Túatha Dé Danann, but he was an absolute sex god nonetheless. He seemed to know exactly when to pick up the pace. His fervent tempo was just as passionate as the desire I felt flowing between us.

Quickly he reached his own climax with a loud shout, and then roughly kissed me. I held onto him tightly as he rode out the waves of his own pleasure, feeling his heart pounding against mine and his breath hot against my skin.

As we lay there in each other's arms, I felt a range of emotions flooding through me: happiness, satisfaction, and a sense of fulfillment. I felt connected to him at that moment, both physically and emotionally. Gradually, I slipped into a deep state of relaxation, my body and mind completely at ease.

~ Rígán ~

It was late in the afternoon, and mo shíorghra and I were chowing down on a mighty lunch in the lively buzz of Púcaí City. I had found us a deadly spot outdoors, with a view that could knock your socks off. We could take in the heart of the city, spread out like a work of art. From where we were sitting, we could spy the wee ponds scattered all over the cityscape, bursting with life, from tiny fishes to lively dragonflies.

And all around us, the púcaí were going about their merry business, filling the air with laughter and banter, creating a sense of camaraderie and good craic.

I savored every single mouthful, delighting in the fresh and wholesome flavors of our extravagant feast. The spread was a sight to behold, with juicy fruits, crispy veg, and mouth-watering cheeses, all arranged on a beautifully-crafted wooden table, adorned with delicate blooms and lush greenery.

The table itself was balanced on a sturdy tree stump base, carved with impressive skill and adorned with fancy designs. The craftsmanship was bleeding top-notch, reflecting the care and talent of its creator. The natural beauty of the wood and the intricacy of the carving added a touch of magic to our dining experience.

As we sat there, surrounded by the buzz of the city and the laughter of the púcaí, I couldn't help but feel grateful for the moment. It was a feast for the senses, a celebration of good food, good company, and the vibrant spirit of Púcaí City.

"Why did you want Ronan so badly?" Moira asked, completely out of the blue, but it was clear that this question had been brewing in her mind for a while.

"What?" I blurted out, caught off guard.

"It seemed like turning Ronan into a púca was very important to you and I wanted to know why," she casually said, while calmly enjoying her meal.

"Sure, that's a bit sudden, mo bhuanghrá, but grand," I drawled, taking a moment to gather my thoughts. "Can't rightly say when I myself turned into a púca, it was bleeding ages ago, but I do remember the fear our old king instilled and how much he fecking despised anything to do with humans. To him, they were just a means of having a bit of craic. Mind you, in his time, human babies were often offered to the púcaí by their own kin for a good riddance.

When I took the throne in the 17th century, as humans count it, I had already lived for centuries in Tír na nÓg. During that time, I saw many changes in the human realm, but very few in ours. Though I always found humans fascinating, their constant evolution since I was a wee one, handed over to the Aes Sídhe, puzzled me.

That's when I realized that creating new púcaí would not only boost my own magical strength with their abilities, but it would also help me understand the human world better through their knowledge of it. One shouldn't underestimate the grasp a child has on its surroundings. Unfortunately, most Aes Sídhe are limited in their power to transform humans into one of us. The most efficient way is to work the magic on infants.

I also saw creating new púcaí as a way to protect the magic of Tír na nÓg, even as the human world moved forward and evolved. As the world around us became more advanced, I knew we had to fecking adapt to keep ahead of the game. Making new púcaí would ensure that our magical power remained strong and significant.

Now, mind you, I'm not one to snatch babies from loving families, like some gobshites might do. I only offer this life to those who have none left, as their loved ones have already given them up to me. Sadly, as fewer humans believe in the Aes Sídhe, or even know what the púcaí are, it's been nearly half a damn century since I last created a new púca."

"So, you get stronger with every púca you create and through that process you're able to learn about what's going on in the human world they came from," she summarized.

"Aye, mo shíorghra," I beamed, delighted with her shrewdness.

"What about Boarder Babies?" she asked, as if the phrase meant something to me.

"Jaysus, what in the name of all that's holy are Boarder Babies?" I blurted out, completely gobsmacked.

"Essentially, Boarder Babies are infants under the age of one who are left in the care of hospitals, often for days or even weeks after birth or later, because their parents or caregivers are either unable or unwilling to take care of them," she explained, her voice filled with emotion. "And let me tell you, it's a truly heartbreaking situation. These little ones find themselves alone in the hospital, without any family or loved ones to comfort them, until they can be placed with a foster care provider."

As far as I knew, hospitals and orphanages were bleeding everywhere in the 20th century, but they weren't exactly the best source of babies for the Aes Sídhe. They were usually so packed that snatching a babe without getting caught was fecking impossible, and most púcaí didn't have the guts or the smarts to pull it off. I couldn't be gallivanting around all the damn time, after all.

I knew that foster care was becoming more popular than orphanages in some places, but since it was a more recent thing, I didn't have much knowledge about the bleeding specifics.

"It's a tough reality to face," she continued. "Many of these babies end up remaining in the foster care system for the rest of their lives. They don't get the chance to experience a stable and permanent home. And here's the thing, some of them face serious health challenges right from the moment they're born. They might have debilitating

health issues, birth defects, or other complications that make it incredibly difficult to find suitable long-term homes for them."

"Is there anyone specifically dedicated to addressing this issue?: I asked. "Making sure they receive love and care?"

"You see, the foster care system strives to provide a nurturing and safe environment for children who cannot live with their biological parents," Moira explained with a heavy heart and a deep sigh. "But when it comes to Boarder Babies, it can be an uphill battle. The fact that they're so young and often have complex medical needs makes it even more challenging to find families who are equipped to provide the specialized care and attention they require. The sad truth is that some of these precious infants don't make it. The mortality rates among Boarder Babies can be alarmingly high due to their fragile health conditions. It's truly devastating to think about the struggles they face right from the start of their lives."

"Are there unwanted infants loitering in hospitals or fecking languishing in foster care then?" I inquired, already contemplating the implications. "Is this a common thing?"

"I mean I don't know the numbers or what it looks like everywhere in the world, but yeah it happens more than I'd like to think." she begrudgingly admitted, her face filled with sorrow.

"Listen, how can you tell if a nipper comes from a caring home but ends up in the hospital, or if they're left all fecking alone in the world?" I asked, genuinely curious. "What's the difference between foster homes and orphanages?"

"I mean, I don't know… but if you can convince me that the life they'd have here was better than the one they would have otherwise, I'd help you figure it out." She promised, reaching across the table to clasp my hand.

"I'm pretty damn sure I can pull that off, mo bhuanghrá," I boasted, overflowing with confidence that I could give them better chances beyond the damn earthly realm.

~ Moira ~

After lunch, Rígán and I strolled hand in hand through the wooded area near the lake, the very spot where I had first encountered Caer. It was a leisurely walk, allowing us to fully immerse ourselves in the breathtaking beauty that surrounded us. The trees that stood tall and graceful created a gentle canopy above, allowing rays of sunlight to filter through and create a mesmerizing dance of light and shadow on the ground beneath our feet.

Every now and then, we would pause to appreciate the captivating scenery before us. We found ourselves enchanted by the interplay of sunlight on the lake's calm surface, as if nature itself had painted a masterpiece. The reflections of the bright sky and fluffy clouds mirrored themselves flawlessly in the serene depths, giving the impression that the heavens had descended to embrace the earth.

As we continued our walk, we were serenaded by the gentle rustling of leaves and the distant calls of birds, a harmonious symphony that blended seamlessly with the peaceful atmosphere. Occasionally, a vibrant butterfly would flutter by, gracing us with a vivid display of colors and adding a touch of magic to the tranquil landscape.

"Today's been really nice," I sighed, stealing a glance at Rígán.

"But?" he countered with a playful smirk, pulling me in for a hug.

"But," I hesitated, "I need you to take this collar off so we can move forward on more equal footing and I need you to work hard to earn my trust back."

"I was hoping you'd be used to the collar by now," he snarked and I felt the weight of it lift off my neck. "Sure, it was a pure beaut, especially on you."

"Too soon," I told him, grinning wryly as I pushed out of the embrace.

"Mo shíorghra, it's never too soon to tell you how bleeding amazing I think everything about you is," he drawled, oozing with charm.

"Look," I started to babble. "I know you can feel how I feel about you through our bond, so you likely already know, but I'm falling for you hard, whether I like it or not - though to be clear I'm not mad about it at this very second. But if we're going to work out, trust and respect will need to go both ways all the time. Sure, there will be breakdowns in communication or just plain misunderstandings, that's life. Every relationship has its ups and downs, adding in magic can't make that easier. Also, I've never really been in a long-term relationship, let alone one that might literally last an eon, but I've seen enough great relationships, like Baz and Lex's, to know it takes constant work, realignment, and compromise. We're going to need to revisit Caer Ibormeith's prophecy about them soon. Ope, shit, I just realized none of those relationships were built while also ruling a city or learning how to live in another civilization. Plus, I'm going to have to learn magic at some point."

"Ease up, ease up," Rígán laughed as I took a breath, pulling me tightly back into him. "You're getting all worked up, mo shíorghra. I'm dead set on making you happy and sticking by your side no matter what, even if it fecking means tearing down all of Tír na nÓg and going head-to-head with ancient damn gods and goddesses. Though, I'd rather avoid such bleeding extreme measures. Personally, I prefer lots of shagging and open communication, but whatever floats your boat."

"Right now," I murmured into his chest, "all I want is to be happy with you."

An Deíreadh?[86]

---

[86] The End?

Epilogue

~ An Morrígan ~

I perceive the tapestry of futures with a clarity surpassing that of Caer Ibormeith. Indeed, unraveling the potential paths that the noble Túatha Dé Danann might traverse proved to be a formidable endeavor. Yet, for me, it was never an insurmountable feat to catch a glimpse of the myriad possibilities that lay ahead, unfurling like a grand symphony.

Caer Ibormeith, a woman whose spirit resonates with mine, how I long for her to possess the heart of a valiant warrior. She required but a gentle push to finally soar into the heavens, embracing the wildness she had missed so dearly.

Securing Boann's temporary assistance, as if she possesses the ability to craft one of my cherished Bean Sí, proved to be a task effortlessly accomplished. The prospect of securing aid for the delight and contentment of her dear young son proved abundantly persuasive, and she graciously extended her assistance, like a benevolent queen bestowing her favor.

The ever so 'magnanimous' and cherished an Dagda, still ensnared by his love for Boann and his fierce protectiveness towards his youngest son, merely awaited the request from the right person to align himself with my hidden cause. And with the proper approach, he readily fell into line.

In due course, when the opportune moment had presented itself, I may have 'inadvertently' divulged a fabrication concerning a plausible, albeit disheartening, future wherein the Young Son and the sacred Yew Berry failed to find solace in each other's embrace. Consequently, he would have traversed the remaining expanse of his existence, burdened with acrimony toward his kith and kin for their incessant intercession, shunning the very presence of Boann, as well as the entirety of his lineage, all the while lamenting the irrevocable forfeiture of his ardor and felicity.

I must confess, I do derive great pleasure from the occasional spectacle, as long as the burden of misfortune does not befall upon my own shoulders.

If fate, in its boundless wisdom, has seen fit to grace me with an intimate comprehension of the profound anxieties that beset the 'esteemed' Boann, in her fearsome contemplation of a potential diminishment in her son's affection for her, it would be the height of folly for me to squander such sacred knowledge. Nay, I would be remiss in my duty were I to disregard its potent influence and fail to wield it to my utmost advantage at the opportune moments that I deem fit.

Moira, my newest Bean Sí and soon-to-be invaluable champion, executed her role with flawless precision. She not only captured the heart of Rígán but also ensnared his mind and loyalty. In no time, their combined power would rival that of any deity.

Ah, it appeared excessively effortless to maneuver the game according to my whims and fancies. So why, pray tell, had I not undertaken such endeavors heretofore? Indeed, the elements were serendipitously aligned as never before, yet numerous instances had transpired wherein the cards were expertly stacked in my favor.

In the beginning, there existed a multitude of viable paths that led resolutely to triumph, engendering an almost undeniable adoration from my subjects. I harbored an unswerving certainty that the pinnacle of felicity lay within my grasp. Alas, it was not meant to materialize. Whenever I stood upon the precipice of attaining my coveted objective, that prospect seemed to wilt away and expire right before my very eyes.

No matter how diligently I exerted myself, the underlying cause eludes my comprehension hitherto.

Verily, I strive with utmost devotion to embody the esteemed role of the Great Queen, as my people so ardently longed for and deserved. Alas, they incessantly yearned for and spurned the visage of a war deity.

I bear no greater affection for any singular aspect of my essence, but rather, I yearn to be perceived and cherished in my entirety. To not be reproached for the facets that reside within me, darker and more formidable than the rest, particularly when they are ceaselessly employed to safeguard my people.

Perchance, I should desist from regarding them as 'my people'. Indeed, I too am of the illustrious Túatha Dé Danann, yet they shall forever remain solely anointed as the people of an Dagda.

They adore him unconditionally; it appears he can commit no transgressions in their discerning eyes. However, it is not his might that consistently delivers them from perilous situations. It is, in fact, my connection with him that brings about such extraordinary achievements.

Would they hold me in higher esteem if they were compelled to implore my assistance, rather than simply seeking it from an Dagda? Alas, it is with a heavy heart that I declare the insignificance of those prospective destinies in this present moment. The notion of those futures, once deemed plausible, has now faded into the realm of impossibility for me.

The benevolent affections of the Túatha Dé Danann shall never grace my being. I am resigned to the solemn reality of beholding naught but terror reflected in their gaze as they cast their eyes upon me. Yet, I shall no longer endure their apprehension and loathing while remaining bound to their revered Great Father.

Erelong, aided by Rígán and Moira, the Túatha Dé Danann shall come to comprehend the true essence of my being, the ethereal Phantom Queen that I am.

Pray, how shall I acquire the assistance of Moira and Rígán, you may inquire?

Rígán, with unwavering devotion, shall undertake any endeavor that ensures the utmost safety and happiness of fair Moira. And the enchanting Moira herself shall exert considerable efforts to preserve her beloved Baz and Lex.

However, this intricate narrative, my dear interlocutor, is a chronicle reserved for a future rendezvous.